Saturday Night
in the
Prime of Life

Saturday Night in the Prime of Life

A Novel
by Dodici Azpadu

AUNT LUTE BOOK COMPANY
IOWA CITY, IOWA
1983

Printed in the United States of America
First Edition

ISBN 0-918040-03-7

Typesetting and book design by Annie Graham.
Printed by the Iowa City Women's Press.
Bound by A Fine Bind.

Cover design by Alexis Kuhr.

Acknowledgments

I am sincerely grateful for the generous help, encouragement, and expertise of all who contributed to the publication of this novel. In addition to the three or four women with whom I worked personally, I appreciate the many others involved in the typesetting, editing, proofing, printing, and design of the book.

one

On a bench in Washington Square Park, facing a New York University building, two women sat arm to arm, hip to hip, thigh to thigh. The younger woman sat with both hands pushing the pockets of her jacket. Its upturned collar protected her neck and ears from the late autumn wind which forced sheets of discarded newspaper and other debris against full garbage barrels, bench legs and wired tree trunks. She was hatless, but the deep collar left unprotected only her olive, hair-downy face and the top of a tangle of tight, black curls cut very short. She held a cigarette in the side of her mouth, a pose that because of her youth straddled the ridiculous and endearing. Her name was Neddie, a diminutive of the Sicilian name she despised.

Her companion, on whose lap was a pile of books, wore a matching scarf and cloche—handmade gifts from her sensible, nordic, midwestern mother. She was Lindy, a graduate student at the university she had always dreamed of attending. In a few weeks it would be 1950, but for Lindy, more than a new decade was approaching. She stared at her gloved hands folded atop the books, and she was conscious of the incongruity between her prim posture and the nagging sexual urgency she felt. "The park isn't very hospitable today," she said.

The thin trees were naked of leaves; pigeons waddled from bench to bench; the dampness increased the bite of the falling temperature. "If it snows on us, we'll get clitoral pneumonia," Neddie commented. "What makes you so sure your roommate is home?"

"Even if no one is there now, what's the point? You know someone could come home at any moment."

"The urge to climb all over you right here in the park should not make me miserable," Neddie mumbled. "It should feel wonderful to be in love."

"I know," Lindy agreed, the wetness in her underpants becoming unpleasantly cold.

"If we don't find some way to be together, I'm afraid it will make us irritable and mean with each other."

"Is that what happens to you?" Lindy's green eyes were wide with surprise and disbelief. She was too newly infatuated to see that frustrated desire had already piqued Neddie.

Neddie smiled around her cigarette. The innocence rather pleased her; Lindy was several years older. She waved her hands to indicate vacancy. She could think of no way to express her ambivalence about searching out relatively secure places to stand with a lover. She was twenty-one, and since high school, she had not been able to accumulate enough money serving and bussing at the café where she had met Lindy to move from her parents' home in Brooklyn. She felt childish and ashamed because she could not offer Lindy a private and secure bed.

As a schoolgirl she had never been allowed to stay overnight at a friend's. And never had she asked anyone to sleep over at her parents' home. From a very early age, her sexual predilections had been obvious to her family. She would not subject a friend to the harangues she endured. Her parents' home was, therefore, unthinkable, even as a last resort.

Lindy's own expensive but run-down apartment usually housed two, sometimes three other women, all of whom Neddie referred to as

2

"your roommate," as though there were only one. On Lindy's single bed, which was only a few feet from another single bed in what had once been a livingroom, they had—fully clothed—tested the limits of restraint. Neddie felt too self-conscious around what she sardonically called "the college educated" to stay with Lindy when roommates were present. And it seemed that roommates and their guests were always coming and going.

This dilemma was familiar to Neddie, but she was afraid to admit it. Every new obstacle to satisfaction threatened her standing in Lindy's affection — or so she believed, based on previous experience. By being mysteriously evasive and—as a consequence of unacknowledged powerlessness—moody, she minimized the difficulties involved until those she was initiating recognized them for themselves. "What I used to do," Neddie said with authority, answering a question Lindy had been asking for days, "would not be right for us. You're not like that."

"For godsake, Neddie! Believe me, I'm like that." Lindy was surprised at her enthusiasm for pleasures, the inclination toward which she had only weeks before discovered.

Forced by Lindy's boldness, Neddie said, "It always seems cheap trying to love someone in an alley or doorway, constantly looking over your shoulder." The admission embarrassed Neddie, who was mildly annoyed with Lindy for requiring that words be put to such necessities.

Lindy, for her part, was evaluating this information. "But we can do it standing up?"

Neddie discarded the stub of her cigarette and stalled for poise. "Do what?"

"Whatever it is we do!" Lindy's sexual honesty was like nothing Neddie had ever experienced. Even when they had talked before, Lindy was never ashamed of what she had or had not done, unlike Neddie, for whom both experience and inexperience were a source of embarrassment.

"Yes," Neddie finally admitted. "We can do it standing up."

"Well, come on," Lindy directed, getting up. "Don't worry, we're not going to do it here. Come on. I know where we can go."

•

C armello Zingaro, barrel-chested, still narrow at the hips, wiry gray patches accentuating the unruly coarseness of his black hair, was the first of Concetta's sons. Except for his name, a flamboyance in speech and gesture when he was excited, and the darkness of his skin, Concetta considered him thoroughly Americanized.

Americanization, when it pleased Concetta, resulted from Carmello's excellence at sports, his seniority in the construction union, and his marriage to a pale but sturdy mid-western girl. Ultimately, americanization rested on Carmello's children — more golden than olive-skinned. In spite of herself, americanization did not always please Concetta. She frequently suffered a racial vertigo, the consequence of gradually bleeding to death — not from the public wound, but from one secretly self-inflicted. Her mixed feelings were obscured by this vertigo so, following a logic of her own, Concetta attributed her son's cultural anemia to unfortunate placement in the birth order of her children. Her first son had been preceded by his sister, Neddie.

Fleshy upper arms folded across the black dress she wore in every weather since the death of her husband, Concetta watched Carmello turn thick hamburger patties on the outdoor grill. Dodging the aromatic smoke, he held the attention of three men who were dressed, as he was dressed, in red and white softball uniforms. The yard was rapidly filling with his teammates, neighbors, and co-workers. These guests, with their wives and children, now outnumbered the early arrivals around whom Carmello's forty-fifth birthday party had grown. As Carmello finished speaking, a burst of laughter erupted. With pleasure Concetta observed other guests in the yard smiling approval in her son's direction.

As she savored Carmello's importance, Concetta noticed him transfer uncooked chicken from a heaping platter to the grill. *Figliu mi!* Concetta thought, as a piece of chicken slipped from the cooking tongs and fell to the ground. She watched her son continue his conversation, recover the meat with his fingers, and inspect it carelessly. Where is Justine? Concetta worried. It's his birthday. He ran around all morning like a boy; he should be resting, not cooking.

4

"Momma, would you like some more ice for your lemonade?" Justine said, wheeling the well-stocked cart to her mother-in-law's shaded chair.

"*Aspiettu!* Leave your wagon," Concetta said, moving both hands in the direction Justine should take. "In front of your friends he's throwing food on the ground."

Justine looked toward her husband, who was now brushing the meat with his fingers. "The germs will burn to death when he puts it on the grill," Justine answered, ignoring Concetta's directive. Before Justine turned away, she saw her husband place the chicken on a paper plate his daughter held below it.

·

"Let me have it, Dad. I'll wash it off at the hose."

"So formal with your old man? Did you just get here?" To his three companions Carmello said, "This is my oldest: Angela. She made me a grandfather two years ago."

Angela would have preferred a private moment with her father; she never knew when he might tease her. But as it was his birthday, she felt obliged to greet him before his position as host and guest of honor made him inaccessible. Salvaging the chicken eased her way. She smiled tentatively at her father's teammates, thinking reserve confirmed her adulthood. Then she quickly excused herself.

"No kisses? No hugs?" Carmello asked when Angela returned with the rinsed chicken breast.

Dutifully, Angela kissed Carmello's cheek and wished him a happy birthday. One of the men to whom Carmello had been speaking walked off to serve himself from a large tub filled with ice, beer, and soft drinks. The other two turned away and took up conversation together. When did she get airs? Carmello wondered. He put an arm around Angela's waist, drawing her closer. "Did you see the game?" he asked. Angela nodded, but did not encourage him to retell his successes. Carmello felt the resistance in his daughter's body and released her with a slap on the hip. "Go say hello to your mother."

·

"I wonder, did she bring the baby?" Concetta asked, but Justine was already pushing the serving cart to three women her own age, wives of Carmello's teammates. They look like a bowl of candies, Concetta noticed, judging the frosted and bleached hair-do's, the even suntans, the starved figures. Lime green, baby pink, and yellow halters or tube tops mixed with blue or white slacks and shorts. They welcomed Justine enthusiastically. "Your husband was full of heroics today," one said. "You missed a good game."

"Wonderful," Justine laughed. "He doesn't have such aches and pains when they win." Their voices blurred in the laughter from another cluster of women in the yard. Concetta, who was not sensitive to boisterous women, nonetheless frowned at the loudness. When she returned her attention to the nearby threesome, Justine was rolling her cart elsewhere.

Momentarily, Concetta was without focus, and vague panic rose in her. True, she had been made comfortable, distinctively comfortable, with her own table and umbrella, but she felt alone. Her teenaged grandson, Carmello, was sitting on the grass a few feet from her, but Concetta had resisted the naive friendliness of the young girl who was with him. The boy himself, never talkative or outgoing, returned a word or two with his friend, but for the most part Concetta's circle was silent. To ease her sense of separateness, Concetta took initiative. Addressing her grandson, but not so pointedly as to embarrass herself if he merely nodded, she said, "How big of your father to invite his players and their families."

As though he had received a compliment and was obliged to diminish it, the young Carmello replied, "They often barbecue after the game. But not always with so much food or so many people."

"Since it's his birthday, I wonder your mother didn't insist on something smaller, just for the family."

"That's not much of a party." He turned his father's eyes on her and explained, "My aunts would have a long commute."

Startled for a moment, Concetta thought the boy was speaking of his aunt Neddie. But Concetta quickly remembered that Neddie, Concetta's oldest, was only a name to him; he had never met her. Young Carmello was speaking of his American relatives. His mother's sisters and their families stayed with Justine and Carmello whenever vacations, conventions, or special events, like Angela's wedding, brought them east from Indiana. Those people were real to the boy. Concetta had met them, of course, but they were not real to her, and she was grateful they lived out-of-state.

Usually Concetta did not attend parties or small gatherings unless she was the hostess or guest of honor. Even so, with her only sister gone, so shortly after her husband — may they rest in peace — Concetta no longer went to the trouble of Sunday dinner. Though three generations lived within driving distance, they all orbited around their own families.

Concetta adjusted the umbrella that shaded her. With a festive paper plate, from which she had eaten neat squares of soft cheese on rye crackers, she fanned the perspiration at her temples. Always her face was carefully powdered, but inexplicably Concetta let her neck and matronly cleavage show the natural, darker color of her skin. As she fanned, her eyes passed over the increasing number of guests. She enjoyed watching the groups form and re-form; she imagined their conversations. Presently, her eyes fixed on Justine and Angela.

Justine, wearing a yellow sun dress that exposed her suntanned shoulders and back, exercised regularly and was thinner than her twenty-year-old daughter. Angela, also wearing a minimal sun dress, was, at the distance from which Concetta observed, hardly distinguishable from her mother. Only her posture, compared to Justine's confidence, revealed her crankiness.

•

Caught in the exuberance of welcoming friends, Justine felt jarred by her daughter's voice and presence. She studied the slate walk on which they both stood, her attention divided between party responsibilities and Angela's claim on her. While the unfamiliar and formal "Mother!" faded from consciousness, Justine controlled her impatience and listened to her daughter. "What does he expect me to do?" Angela was saying. "Fall all over him? He has the whole silly team to do that."

"His little girl is special." Once she spoke, Justine knew the formula was wrong; she added weakly, "Appreciation means more from family." Angela had already stiffened. Justine adjusted the top of her dress, which seemed to slip as her own bosom was reflected in her daughter's petulant heaving.

"It's all flattery."

7

"We can't talk now, Angela. If it's flattery, it's harmless. It's his birthday."

"Every day is his birthday."

"Not now, Angela. Will you say hello to Granma? She shouldn't be alone. Your brother is probably restless by now. Uncle Bobo is not here yet; he usually sits with her."

"First he sends me to you, then you send me to her!"

Why didn't she bring the baby? Justine wondered. She released the serving cart, and with a sigh she wound her arms around her daughter. "Baby," she said. Then closing her eyes for concentration, "Angela, darling, I'll talk to you later, after we get the party underway. I'm glad you came early; I need your help. I'd be annoyed if he slapped me in public, too."

"You'd be more than annoyed," Angela said, trying to step back and restate her complaint.

"Can this wait, Angela? Will you help me?" Justine did not open her embrace until she felt her daughter surrender to it.

"Oh, Mom," Angela said, abashed by receiving the comfort she had sought. She averted teary eyes from her mother's persistent gaze. "Okay. I'll help. Let me go."

Concetta dissolved the troubling image of Justine and Angela entwined, but instantly she brightened as she saw her Carmello approach with a small crispy spare rib squeezed in the cooking tongs. He kissed her heartily and offered the food. "To hold you until the serious eating begins. We're filling all the kids with hamburgers first."

With animation Concetta said, "Why aren't you sitting? Justine or Angela can do that. You ran around all morning." And showing more affection for her grandson than she felt, Concetta continued, "Carmello here came for me early and took me to the game. We left before the end, though. Justine forgot to buy the ice for the party."

"She didn't forget," Carmello junior defended his mother. "You can't very well buy the ice in advance." He swallowed his exasperation and turned to his father. "You played a great game, Dad."

"Yes, you did!"

Carmello turned to beam at the compliment of his son's friend. The boy mumbled an introduction. "Dad, this is Ann. We play together in the orchestra."

"Happy birthday, Mr. Zingaro," the girl said, relieved to be in friendlier company.

"It's okay to kiss me," Carmello said, not releasing Ann's hand. "I don't play in the orchestra."

"Your father is still something with the ladies," Concetta laughed. Young Carmello looked away as Ann ransomed her hand with a kiss. He was relieved to see his sister joining them. Everyone watched Angela bend to kiss Concetta's cheek.

"Hi, Granma," she said. "I see it's cooler here in the shade." Concetta gestured with her chin.

Taking Ann's hand and nervously brushing it, young Carmello said, "This is my older sister Angela. This is Ann."

"I thought Carr was the oldest," Ann said smiling.

"Lots of people think so," Angela admitted, her own smile uncurling. "I don't know why."

" 'Cause I'm the first in looks," said the acne-plagued Carmello.

"Just like his father," Concetta added, misunderstanding the pacifying intent of her grandson's remark.

"Is my father better looking than Aunt Neddie?" Angela asked, exaggerating innocence. The older Carmello, having felt one of his son's inexplicable mood changes, and also wanting to avoid his daughter, had returned to the barbecue grill before Angela spoke. Now the younger Carmello, wrapping Ann's hand with his own, excused them both.

"You chased everyone away, *cacadda.*"

"The men in the family have short attention spans." Angela watched her brother and his date, relieved of further responsibility for social lubrication, settle themselves in a tree-shaded part of the yard.

"Did you forget the baby?"

"How could I forget a baby?"

"Who knows these days. Young people do strange things."

"William is working till three. I was lucky to find a sitter even for a few hours on such a gorgeous day. He'll pick up the baby on his way here."

"After he works all day you make your husband take care of the baby?"

Angela's husband had made a similar objection, but Angela answered her grandmother as though she and William were of one mind. "Why not? I work all week and take care of the baby."

"See what I mean? In my time we never left any of you with a stranger. Your mother brought you to *me* when she had to go out; her own mother was so far away. But I accepted you like you were my own." Concetta did not modify her statement; she added absently, "*Non rispiettu.*"

"This is still 'in your time,' Granma."

"Not for long. Still it doesn't pay to complain. I'll be left with only this umbrella to talk to."

Angela sighed and lapsed into silence. It would have been easier with the baby. She had little in common with the other guests, though they regularly appeared at her parents' entertainments. Angela did not like her grandmother, but sitting with her was sanctioned, even praiseworthy. Until William arrived she would surrender herself to that security.

In an effort to be agreeable, Concetta patted Angela's hand. "Don't rush into another. Children take up your whole life, and what for?"

Angela was familiar with her grandmother's mixture of maternal pride and maternal cynicism. "Believe me, I don't want another."

"No. No. Just one . . . is not right. People could think there was something wrong in your marriage. I meant only not to rush. Enjoy your life. Grow up yourself."

"I only want one," Angela insisted.

"You'll see. After a while you'll want to give your William a son."

Angela shifted her chair to gain the direct rays of the sun. Her legs were still in the shaded circle that Concetta's umbrella created, but she closed her eyes to enjoy the sun and to avoid her grandmother's advice. She did eventually want a son, but from habit she disagreed with Concetta.

"Your uncle must be caught in traffic," Concetta said. Angela disliked it when people emphasized her relationship to a family member rather than their own. Concetta could have said, "My son, Bernardo" or just "Bobo"—which is what everyone called him anyway. Saying "your uncle" somehow made Angela responsible for his absence. She showed her annoyance by exchanging a look with Concetta which suggested that they both knew better than to suppose Bernardo was in traffic.

•

Justine and Carmello, arm in arm at the yard gate, waved good-bye to the last of their guests. Justine was satisfied by the abundance she had been able to provide for so many friends on such a lovely day. "Well, Mr. Forty-five, how did you like your party?"

"I ate too much cake," Carmello answered, folding a canvas chair. "You do every year."

Together Justine and Carmello gathered and stacked outdoor furniture. They worked in silence for a time, each savoring the echoes of a yard full of cheerful, appreciative friends. "Everyone had a good time," Carmello declared.

"I think so. Exhausted?" The yard was cleared of chairs. Justine handed Carmello folded garbage bags from a supply near the back door of the house.

"I'm okay." The residue of excitement prevented Carmello from recognizing the extent of his fatigue. He followed Justine around the yard, holding a bag open to receive used paper cups and plates and empty bottles and cans. "You missed some wonderful baserunning this morning. I played like I was nineteen." Too bad Bobo missed it, Carmello thought, he loves sports. "Who took my mother home?"

"Angela and William. Angela was with her most of the afternoon. I'm afraid your mother was bored. I could only get to her in snatches. I was counting on Bobo. I'm surprised he hasn't called."

"My mother doesn't exactly put herself out to speak to anyone she hasn't known all of her life. Or all of theirs." Justine was silent. "Bobo must still be frying in traffic. You don't think he didn't come because of the ice between his wife and momma, do you?" Justine, who thought so, shook her head. Carmello continued, "I don't know why he still lives in the city. He could be closer to us. There's a breeze now. Good sleeping weather." Carmello stopped following Justine and thought about his brother's absence.

Justine gathered the few remaining paper plates and carried them to her husband. She knew his feelings were hurt because the usual place his younger brother gave him had been pre-empted by a family quarrel between women. Carmello did not often suffer secondary importance. Justine decided to distract him from a potential sulk. Striking him hard, she raised the dust on his softball pants.

He nearly dropped the garbage bag. "What's that for?"

"Your daughter," Justine said. "Be grateful I waited until everyone is gone. Your daughter is a grown woman. I don't want to see you slapping her ass again."

"You like it when I slap your ass."

"I'm serious, Carmello. Do you understand me? You embarrassed her."

"She embarrassed me first."

"Do you understand me?" Justine poked Carmello's bicep with a single, sharp, polished fingernail. She had made up her mind to speak about the incident despite Angela's whiny complaint, despite her own desire for her husband. Effortlessly affectionate while the children were young enough to adore him, Carmello was baffled by their maturation. He would never say so; yet, he felt his charm over them was fading. But Angela had been married for three years; Carr would graduate from high school in a year. The transition with Carr need not be so difficult as it had been with Angela, if Carmello understood that the children's changing toward him did not mean their affection was lessening. Justine did not want Carmello to become self-deluded by loveless formalities as his father had been.

Speaking of the afternoon incident with Angela, especially considering Justine's instinctive timing and tone, did not threaten her desire. Tired as she was, she wanted her husband. She often did after they entertained. Among their friends it seemed to her that everyone wanted him. His teammates and neighbors called him by a variety of nicknames, and those had filled the yard all afternoon. Justine wanted her appreciation of him to be special.

Carmello tied the last of the plastic bags and placed it against the garbage rack. He looked over the tidy yard. "I think I'll water the grass before I come in. It'll help me calm down."

"I'm getting in the tub," Justine said, but she stopped at the screen door. She had watched him from the other side of the screen door that morning. Finishing salads for the party when he returned from the game, she heard him laughing and boasting with his favorites from the team. They had won and that would please him throughout the day. She heard the other men address themselves to him, measuring their comments against a standard he set. Immediately, she wanted to bite the gray and black hairs clustered above the vee of his uniform shirt and claim him for herself. During the day, women at the party remarked how trim and boyish Carmello looked, how devoted to his family and to Justine he was. Not like their husbands, who wore their pants under their rounded stomachs and had to be prodded as hosts, and even as guests.

Now as Justine stood at the back door watching Carmello fanning the water spray toward the thick hedges that bordered their property, she was grateful for all his labor provided. He satisfied her dreams for a virile, but docile, husband, a comfortable home, a secure, enviable family life. Carmello actually enjoyed her company, as well as the pleasures and responsibilities of entertaining. He took pride in their home, in her.

The temperate May nightfall was coming quickly when Justine moved to press her body against Carmello's back. "You are as dear to me now, Mr. Birthday, as on our wedding day."

"I knew you were back there."

"How did you know?"

"I can always feel when someone is watching me."

"You get lots of practice."

"I'm a lucky man to have you." He looked down and could barely see Justine's fingers undoing the buttons of his uniform pants. "What are you up to?"

"I'm helping you water the grass. I don't want you to take too long."

"Keep that up and I won't take long at all."

"No. I want to bathe. Just don't take too long."

Carmello twisted the nozzle closed, and as he turned to his wife, he let the hose fall to the ground.

"Not here, silly."

"Why not?" Carmello's hands were quickly under Justine's dress.

"It's not even fully dark. Carmello!" But Carmello was already preparing his welcome. "Someone could hear us."

"It's our backyard." Holding her close, both of them giggling and whispering, Carmello led his wife to a redwood divan he had rolled to a protected part of the yard.

"Let's go inside."

"I want to do it out here. It's my birthday." Carmello urged Justine to lie back on the divan as he held her thighs and lost his face between her legs. As she became more and more expressive, he put the side of his hand in her mouth. Justine sucked and bit on Carmello's palm and tried to hurry her own pleasure. Her husband rested a moment before he said, "Take this off."

"Out here? What *is* the matter with you?"

13

"Was something the matter with me?" He helped Justine edge the light dress over her head and shoulders. In the moonless dark he appreciated what he could see of his wife. Two pregnancies had not altered her firm, round breasts, and she was unwrinkled in the hips and thighs. Concerned that weight gain or signs of aging might affect his enthusiasm for her — even against his will — he inspected her regularly. His compliments were frequent, sincere, and also influential.

After the first shock to her temperature, Justine felt the luxury of being naked out of doors. Nonetheless, she said, "We better go inside before someone calls the police and we're arrested." Modesty was not the only reason Justine pressed for the comfort of the indoors. She hoped the change of site would renew Carmello's enthusiasm for culminating her pleasure.

"We won't be arrested. This is my yard; you're my wife; this is my birthday. I'm not forty-five every day."

Resigned by familar body language to incompletion, Justine graciously subdued the echo of her daughter's observation that every day was Carmello's birthday. She drew him to her. "Okay, cock of the walk, get comfortable."

He exploded almost as soon as he entered her, but Carmello was not concerned. He trusted Justine to restore him and to open herself to him in the ways that pleased him. Defusing her own dissatisfaction, Justine was thorough in the pleasures she gave. Her own expertise and Carmello's gratitude fortified her image of herself as attractive and sexually complete. It was nearly midnight when, with clothes in hand, still whispering mischievously about their lark, they went into the house.

two

*W*rought iron bars from the outside gate cast late afternoon shadows into the lobby of the apartment building. The vertical stripes stretched across industrial carpeting and climbed toward a bank of mailboxes, a gilt-filigree mirror, two mock-leather benches, and four artificial areca palms. Confidently indifferent to the lobby décor, an armful of books and looseleaf papers pressed against her, Lindy Russell outdistanced the shadows and rang for an elevator. Alone in the car, she pressed the bundles against the elevator wall and blew a strand of ticklish gray hair away from her nose. The topknot she had worn for years was threatening to uncoil, as it did at the end of every school day. As she worked her key in the apartment door, a stylish purse slipped from her shoulder and dangled from its strap at her knees.

"The pack horse cometh," she said, closing the door with her hip.

She might have called for help, but the habit of independence in her ritual of overburdened arrival and the likelihood of Neddie resting after work prevented her. If Neddie were not asleep, the hint would be sufficient.

Neddie was not asleep, but she did not go to the door. Still in her post office uniform, lunch pail on the oak nightstand she herself had refinished, she sat on the edge of the bed. Tears covered her face. Lindy toppled her books and papers onto the bed. A letter dangled from the limp hand Neddie held at her thigh. On the summer-weight quilt was a torn envelope with a return label Lindy recognized. Rather than thinking the letter was from Neddie's mother, as the label indicated, Lindy assumed news of Concetta Zingaro's passing had arrived. She was not ordinarily inclined to extreme judgments, but in twenty-six years of living with Neddie, Lindy had never seen her so absolutely in tears.

Guessing Lindy's morbid thought, Neddie handed her the single sheet of paper and said, "No. It's not that."

Lindy read the letter carefully to assure herself that no one had died. A further reading clarified what had moved Neddie like an undertow: an admission of loneliness after a family celebration; ordinary, though unexpected, questions about Neddie's well-being; an expression of maternal love; and finally, the unprecedented wish that best regards be given to Neddie's friend. Lindy thought it possible that, from studious and long-standing avoidance, Concetta might actually have forgotten her name. She opened her lips to speak, but closed them without a sound. She began again, but both from surprise and self-censure she was wordless a second time.

Sitting beside Neddie, she put an aged and sun-freckled hand on Neddie's thigh, but this seemed terribly insufficient against tears. "At least you won't drown to death from the inside," she said weakly, then added, "You could talk your thoughts out with the tears?" But she expected no such event.

Neddie cut the sultry air with her open hand: what words could possibly contain all that she might say?

The unwillingness to speak usually made Neddie's tears convulsive. The pain did not frighten Lindy, nor did the reticence irritate her, as both had in the past. Over the years she had seen enough of Neddie's tears and silences — though not recently, it was true — to accept the paradoxical self-control. Neddie's family haunted their life together. Often, to oil the progress of Neddie's awareness (and neglecting the responsibility of her own), Lindy had put Neddie's feelings and thoughts to speech for her. But this letter, considering the communications that preceded it, gagged Lindy too.

Always before she had wondered why, if you cried as volcanically as Neddie cried, would you trouble yourself with the dubious dignity of silence? It had seemed an empty gesture of choking on the truth. Now she understood the meaning of "tongue-tied." The silence was, on the one hand, *imposed* as a consequence of multiple insult; and on the other hand, silence kept the history and scale of the injury intact.

That precious history, Lindy thought, organizing her emotions against Neddie's mother. Unpleasant telephone calls every five or six months. A personal sentence or two squeezed below pre-printed holiday greetings. Occasionally a family picture from which Neddie's once-conspicuous absence now seemed natural. But this letter from home, over which one middle-aged woman sobbed and another sat bitterly mute, was the only one of its kind. There is no other historical evidence, Lindy thought. No documents. No ruins. Nothing tangible against which to compare the ostensibly benign letter and condemn it. It contained nothing but civilized questions and sentiments — a quarter of a century late.

.

Vividly, Lindy recalled carrying boxes, clothes, and furniture from a rented truck to their first apartment. They had driven cross-country with the truck and lived out of it until they found a home. They knew no one in the city and moved entirely alone. The monotonous pace of taking realistic loads up two flights of stairs was relieved only by breaks to accommodate a meter reader and telephone installer. Even during lunch they kept pace by driving to have extra keys cut and making arrangements at the post office. Solely to accomplish the goal of emptying the truck before dark, they worked beyond exhaustion. After nine o'clock, leaving Lindy to drag the remaining unopened boxes to their proper rooms, Neddie went out for pizza.

She returned also carrying wine and a bouquet of daisies from an all-night supermarket. With these she surprised Lindy. Too tired for conversation, they ate less than half of the small pizza; the wine was hardly touched; the flowers, though bright, were clumped in a rusted coffee can they found under the sink. On the naked mattress which had inadvertently been left in the livingroom, still fully dressed they fell asleep in each other's arms.

Early the next morning, still surrounded by boxes and balled newspaper, Lindy opened her eyes to the sight of Neddie holding a cold piece of folded pizza and swallowing from a bottle of red Segesta.

"Breakfast?"

"Not until my mouth starts working," Lindy said, returning Neddie's kiss. "Even the mouth of life's tour guide needs rest. I didn't realize you got pepperone."

"Who could taste anything last night? Sleep okay?"

"Like a baby, but I ache. We should have showered. Look at this mess." Lindy propped herself up to survey the room.

"Don't talk about our happy home that way."

"Thanks for the flowers. Do you suspect that their vase was once used for the toilet bowl brush?"

"Nothing is too good for you."

"Neddie? I'm glad to be here with you."

"Not afraid?" Neddie asked, chewing pizza crust.

"A little, I suppose, but more happy than frightened."

"Unceremonious as it is, I drink to the beginning of our life together." Neddie drank from the bottle and handed it to Lindy, who also drank from it. The exchange of ironies about their conjugal surroundings was interrupted by the unfamiliar telephone ring. "Who on earth can that be?" Neddie questioned, lifting herself stiffly to answer one of the newly installed phones.

Helping herself to a wedge of pizza, Lindy frowned when she heard Neddie on the bedroom phone change in mid-sentence from English to Sicilian. She wondered why Neddie had told her mother where they were going. And how did Concetta get the number so quickly? Unless she had called long distance information every day since Neddie had left New York? The least she can do is wait until we're settled. Lindy listened for a revealing word or two in English. The unmistakable rhythm and tone of argument wound down before the call ended.

Kicking past empty boxes, Neddie returned to the livingroom, sat heavily on the mattress, and lit a cigarette. "That was my father."

"I thought it was your mother."

"Big guns for big occasions. After all, I don't move in with the love of my life every day. He called to assure me that if he were physically well, he would be here to beat me into decency."

"Is that a Sicilian wedding custom, for godsake? And what physically well? Has his mental imbalance spread?"

"He did not specify what prevented him."

"Perhaps his addiction to your mother's fastidious care of his royal person."

"Don't get complacent," Neddie advised. She knew her father's threats were idle. Out of kindness she might have minimized the conversation, but she wanted to provoke Lindy's indignation. She forced a light voice to repeat what she had been told. "He's grooming my brothers to come do the job for him. And we'll never know when they'll turn up."

"Gooning your brothers is more like it. Someone will have to restore their manly Latin honor. What slimy shit."

"You don't know what you're talking about," Neddie answered sharply.

"You don't think he's serious?"

"Not the way you mean. But he's serious all right. Have you ever known him to call me?"

"I've never known him to speak to you." Lindy did not know what had caused the breach in alliance between her and Neddie. "You think one of your brothers is going to travel three thousand miles to break your thumbs?" Neddie made no reply. With her foot, she pushed the coffee can of daisies away from the bed. The cigarette drooped from the corner of her mouth.

Anxious about losing their rapport and inexplicably insecure about her humor, Lindy bounced a piece of pizza crust in and out of the oily cardboard box and resorted to generalizations. "It's slimy bullshit."

"Don't keep saying that."

"You don't think it's ridiculous?"

"Don't keep saying 'slimy.'"

"Why did you tell them where we were going?" Lindy asked with conciliatory softness. Neddie turned her shoulder impatiently, and her moody inaccessibility clouded the first weeks of their domestic life together.

At least that was the end of hearing from Neddie's father, Lindy reminded herself, glancing at the bedroom clock to guess how long Neddie had been crying. Neddie's mother called on every religious holiday, including the feasts of saints with severed breasts and plucked eyes. Mention of Concetta Zingaro stirred a resentment to which Lindy instantly succumbed. Neddie's longsuffering was Lindy's as well. Until his death, Concetta had occasionally renewed her husband's threat; after it, she claimed that Neddie's behavior had killed him. Mostly she relied on her own novenas and curses to save or revile her daughter. Eventually, Lindy acknowledged, the seasonal invectives had dwindled to April and December. But if their intensity and ingenuity had diminished, their effects had not.

Slowly, their fifth Easter together focused for Lindy. *Immersed in an early-morning scented bath when the phone rang, she could not protect Neddie's sleep. She listened unselfconsciously, hoping a friend was suggesting a barbecue for the afternoon or proposing a drive along the coast. She thought she might suggest a drive herself, when the bathroom door, which always stuck, swung open and banged against the stopper.*

"*Who's calling so early?*" *she asked, but she knew by Neddie's expression.*

"*Just my mother reminding me to do my Easter duty and telling me how much she loves me.*"

"*What's your Easter duty?*"

"*If I don't go to confession around this time of year, I'm excommunicated. I don't remember exactly; I haven't made my Easter duty in years.*"

"*She could be more explicit.*"

"*Believe me, she was.*"

"*What did she have to say?*"

"*The usual. Only of course she uses the fact of my not going to church. Today I asked her what was so dirty and disgusting about not going to church. She doesn't go regularly. She said I was making fun of God.*"

"*By not going to church?*"

"*No. I think she meant for asking the question. I was making fun of God by pretending she wasn't talking about sex and sin when she said 'dirty and disgusting.'*"

Watching Neddie sink into annoyance, Lindy said, "Sometimes I think you'd be disappointed if she didn't call and go on like that. Don't you think you take perverse pride in her vehemence?"

Neddie was perversely attached to her mother's calls. They were virtually the only Sicilian she heard or spoke. She assumed that her mother embodied their common racial heritage; and though, through this fragile connection, Neddie was invariably condemned, she stiffened against the threat which Lindy's questions represented. "It isn't important."

Lindy wanted to agree, but she dared not. "Really, Neddie, do you suppose you make too much of her psychological crudities? I mean, she goes on like this year after year. Will you take the bait every time?" Lindy stood in the tub, let the water drain, and covered herself with a large towel.

"Psychological crudities!" Neddie spat toothpaste foam into the sink. "I said it wasn't important."

"It isn't necessary to pass your hurt on to me. It doesn't have to ruin our day." Lindy covered herself in the towel longer than usual when she saw Neddie open the tap so that it splashed over the sink and onto the floor.

Closing the faucet with pipe-squealing speed, Neddie said, "I'm not hurt. And none of it has anything to do with you. Or with our day."

The ridicule in Neddie's last words embarrassed Lindy. Both continued their bathroom routines in silence until Lindy spoke. "Want to drive along the coast? Just the two of us? I'll make a picnic?" She watched Neddie struggle to answer agreeably. Neddie could change quickly from good temper to bad, but once ensnared by bad temper, she could only civilize her depression.

"It's a nice idea," she mumbled, "but I don't feel much like driving."

Determined to be amenable, Lindy added, "Maybe you'll want to go this afternoon."

•

Re-experiencing the old shame of her placating voice, Lindy remembered that they did not drive along the coast that Easter Sunday. They read the newspapers; they watched television, napped, ate meals; they occupied the same rooms, but each was quite alone.

Lindy did not know when she came to envy the twisted caring

evident in Concetta's calls. Her own family had been less passionate in disapproval, but more decisive. It had been many years — more than fifteen? she wondered — since she had flown to Des Moines for Thanksgiving, the lesser fall holiday. She would not sacrifice Christmas with Neddie. Her family knew she had been living with Neddie for some time, but they never invited Neddie for the holiday. The truth is, Lindy admitted, I never even hinted that such an invitation would be appropriate or welcome. How were they to know? Not that their *knowing* would have resulted in an invitation. That was only too clear. Until they became estranged, that yearly visit and perfunctory contact by telephone or letter three or four times a year were the only efforts at communication. Duty, rather than feeling, motivated all parties. Did estrangement energize their connection in some mysterious way? She certainly *felt* more about them after it than before.

Lindy could not remember if it was in her ninth or tenth year with Neddie that her parents vacationed in the West. Their proximity to her life clarified what Lindy suspected: her reluctance to tell about Neddie cut more deeply than anticipated prejudice about sexuality. She lost sleep over their coming; she cried; she argued with herself and with Neddie. But the worst was over after a single, brutally polite meeting.

On an old sheet that protected the camel velour surface of the couch from furniture-refinishing debris, Neddie, in household work clothes, was stretched full-length. Lindy, depleted by an afternoon of sightseeing with her parents, was relieved to find Neddie finished with her work and smiling. "Brace yourself," she said. "My parents have invited you to dinner."

"That's nice."

"You'll go?"

"Why not; you told them about us?"

"Come on, Neddie, we've been through that."

Neddie sat up. "Wish I wasn't so dirty. I want to take you back from their world." Holding her body carefully away from the sanding dust that covered Neddie, Lindy offered herself to be kissed. "I don't care if you tell them. If you don't want to, it should be easy to find a reasonable excuse for my absence."

"Neddie, they want to see where I live. To meet you. This is just the first step. We'll have to invite them to dinner."

"They're welcome in our home."

"You're being difficult." Lindy pulled a cotton dress over her head, draped it over a lampshade a safe distance from the work disorder, and sat beside Neddie.

Wrapping both arms around her friend, Neddie said, "I'm really being very simple. If you don't want to tell them about us, that's okay with me. You know it is. But I won't pretend I'm someone I'm not. On my own time, no less."

"I'll tell them after they meet you. How's that?"

"After they see me, it won't be necessary to tell them."

"But if I tell them first, they won't want to meet you. Then what will have been the point of telling them?"

"Now that's a logical twist worthy of you. If it's such a sure thing, what's the point of going to dinner?"

Lindy did not answer. Did she hope her relationship to Neddie might escape notice if only one or two visits were required? Thanks to geography, there had never been any reason to tell. Her parents might never come west again. Wasn't it unnecessarily disruptive? Had she ever mentioned to them that Neddie was Sicilian? Lindy wondered. Not likely. The vacuum created by conscientious omission on the subject of her home life was boomeranging. She knew her parents suspected that this person called Neddie was actually a man. During her last visit to Des Moines her father, a church elder, had asked about it in his dignified, authoritarian fashion.

If they never have to meet again, she thought, her parents might prefer not to see the obvious in Neddie's short hair style, in the material or cut of her slacks, in her rough confidence. Oh, god, in the endless toothpick substitutes for cigarettes. But even if they could ignore that, could they also ignore what was obvious in her deeply olive complexion, her wiry hair, her face and hand language? She was genuinely gracious, even though she was unorthodox. Lindy sighed; she knew the answers to her questions. Why then was she insisting on a meeting? They invited your roommate to dinner, her mental heckler answered in sing-song; the social forms have caught up with you. After ten years even a roommate has some status. Frustrated tears filled the large green eyes she turned on Neddie. "The invitation is for tonight."

Neddie loosened her embrace. "That's easy enough. I wasn't home to receive it."

"They're coming here to pick us up." Neddie was silent longer than Lindy could bear. In a burst of tears, she added, "It's not my fault I had to lie."

Neddie returned her arm to Lindy's shoulder. "Sweet woman, I know. Don't blame yourself. Sure, you could have told the truth and had no parents, or parents like mine. Don't be ashamed. You did what you thought you could get away with."

"What are we going to do when they come? Are you going out?"

"Come on. Dry your face or they'll think I beat you."

"It makes me sick to drive you out of the house."

"You aren't driving me out of the house." Neddie stared at her dusty pants. "I won't run away from my own home."

"Are you going to hide?"

Neddie's glance criticized Lindy for speaking of what certainly was not a possibility. "I will say 'How do you do?' and pour large glasses of my good scotch. Then I'll talk to your father about this table I'm working on. Then I'll join you all for dinner."

Lindy had no enthusiasm for the victory; tears came in earnest as Neddie comforted her. "One more thing," she said, laughter now mixed with the tears. "They don't drink."

Neddie laughed too. "In that case, I'll pour large glasses of my best scotch. And you'll tell them about us before they come here for dinner?" Aloud Lindy agreed; silently she added the qualification: if necessary.

It had not been necessary; there was no reciprocal dinner. After awkward introductions and painfully slight conversation, Lindy's mother developed a migraine before the dessert course of an expensive dinner for which Neddie was predictably underdressed. The headache necessitated an early disbanding of the party, which no one regretted.

The following evening Lindy's father called. Was she quite aware of the sort of person her friend was? Lindy could still hear the precise words. She could still feel the hesitation and disdain for the word "friend." Quite aware, she had answered with more poise than she had thought herself capable. In that case, unless she speedily ended this appalling and apparently hypnotic relationship with a person so obviously beneath her in so many ways, she was no longer welcome at home.

Neddie had always praised Lindy's reaction to the ultimatum, even after Lindy confessed that shock at the venom of her father's disapproval—not courage—caused the phone to slip from her hand and break the connection. Fear, not indignation, prevented her from dialing him back at his hotel. But as Lindy returned to full consciousness

24

of her surroundings — Neddie undone beside her — she acknowledged the truth anew. It was anger that had curbed any desire to negotiate a compromise during the remaining days of her parents' visit. Gradually she sealed off ways her parents might express a change of heart. They no longer knew where she lived or how to reach her. By these efforts she convinced herself that she was separated from them by choice. She did not know if they ever tried to reach her. She did not know if both were still alive.

Tears from Lindy's past now spilled into mid-life. She rubbed Neddie's leg. "Lie down while I massage your back," she told Neddie, whose shaking sobs had subsided. "Maybe you can cry yourself to sleep." Neddie curled on the bed protecting herself from massage. Silently, but not secretly, Lindy let the re-experienced sadness flow without restraint. She stroked the rough uniform material that covered Neddie's raised hip, and supposed she was grateful for the cleanliness of her parents' decision. There was *nothing* between them. Still, Lindy thought, accepting relief from what was being washed out of her, silence accumulates; its meaning changes over the years. Silence is not nothing.

three

"We've never had much of a view," Neddie said, looking past the rusted iron fire escape to the window-box of begonias across the alley. "How do we always manage rear apartments?"

"You make it sound like being seated in unobtrusive, dark corners at restaurants," Lindy answered, pushing scraps from a dinner plate into the garbage. "Our first apartment faced the street."

"Did it?" Neddie carried two coffee mugs looped in her fingers and a glass coffee pot to the round oak table.

"Don't tell me you're thinking of moving?"

Neddie shook her head emphatically. "Just nostalgia. I feel like something monumental happened last night. Today at work I wondered if it showed somehow that I'd cried for hours during the night. Was I different? I used to wonder 'Did it show?' the day after I started

27

with a new lover. 'Can these strangers tell I've been up all night enjoying myself?'"

Lindy poured coffee for both of them. "You're not *different*. Just accentuating a syllable of yourself that I don't often hear. Very polite. Very measured in speech, like you are sometimes after we've argued."

"Did we?"

"No. You cried yourself to sleep. I cried myself out in the tub."

"I remember undressing in the middle of the night. Felt wonderful to be up so early; before the birds, it seemed. I'm sorry you were alone in the tub. I thought I wanted to be alone, but when you came home I realized it was easier with you there. I think I'm being polite 'cause I don't want to lose contact with you. But I don't have anything to say."

"Sounds like the aftermath of a fight to me." Lindy laughed. She covered Neddie's dark bony curled fingers with her own flecked manicured hand. With the grain of the oak table they formed a pleasing study of textures.

"You think it was between me and my mother?"

"It's not inconceivable. But I'm only guessing."

"I was looking at the old photographs this afternoon, before you came home."

"I'll get them." Lindy's enthusiasm for the photographs, which were primarily of Neddie's family, was not feigned. She too felt something cathartic had happened, and like Neddie she thought the photographic touchstones might elucidate it. She left the table and returned with a shoebox of yellow and white photo envelopes. "Has anyone changed since we last looked?"

"Only me, I think. That's why I was looking. I felt changed, but I don't know how. Here we are in the Caffè Sport," Neddie said, pulling a colored shot from a folder selected at random.

Lindy smiled at the image of herself with a fringed, silk scarf folded once at her throat and hanging asymmetrically against her black blouse. "Who took that?" Not Neddie, who sat beside her in an ornate booth, her hands a blur of movement the camera could not freeze. Together they looked more native to the North Beach caffè than Lindy recalled feeling.

"Remember that fellow I was talking to about black snails and lambs' heads?"

"I don't remember."

"He bought us anisette for our espresso? We talked for nearly an hour, though not much in English. I think you were absorbed in the carvings and the table decorations. The place was elaborately over-done. He took both of these." Neddie held another photo of them posed next to a small, carved and decorated Sicilian cart.

They continued examining scenes from their San Francisco vacation only a few summers past, but these were not the gauges they sought. Concetta's calls were generally preceded by greeting cards in which she not infrequently included pictures of herself with one or the other of her sons. It was these images that Neddie and Lindy periodically used to measure current emotions against past.

"She doesn't change much," Neddie said. They both contemplated a recent picture of Concetta, beaming and upright on a folding chair in front of the family brownstone in Jamaica. Her sons, Carmello and Bernardo, stood on either side of her. Only Carmello is actually handsome, Lindy thought, observing that Bernardo's eyes were on him.

Neddie thumbed several old pictures of her brother and his family, her parents holding their grandson at his christening, an aunt and several cousins at a wedding shower for Angela. In the shots of her immediate family, which Neddie now shuffled quickly, they being so numerous, a similarity of composition was evident. Concetta seated. One or both sons flanking her. Lindy did not resist saying, "Does she have movable parts?"

"She's short. I think she avoids standing. As you can see, she is unable to smile without male attendants. Bobo looks older than she does in this one."

The picture Lindy held hardly differed from several they had already seen. Bernardo, standing to one side of Concetta's garden chair, rested one hand on his mother's shoulder; the other encircled Carmello, who presided in his sunny yard. Both brothers usually posed with hands on hips, legs apart. Pants virtually unzipped, Lindy thought carelessly. In picture after picture, Carmello smiled confidently at the camera. "She could send the same picture every year," Lindy said, rubbing her eyes and yawning.

She knew the Zingaros only from snapshots and stories, and from their effect on Neddie's life and on her own life. Staring at an image of Concetta and her deceased sister, Lindy saw the same deference between Neddie's aunt and mother as between Neddie's brothers. Neddie's aunt nearly duplicated Concetta's features, and that was altogether too much Concetta for Lindy. Concetta's nose, eyes and mouth epitomized an unpleasant racial mixing which only in Neddie did Lindy find attractive. Sour adrenalin turned in her stomach. Fear of how she might be treated by Neddie's family, if there were ever an occasion, included wariness of the deceased aunt as well as prejudice against the brothers. How could she love Sicilian ways in Neddie, yet dislike them in Neddie's family? Lindy shook her head clear of the hypnotic influence of past reactions and fanned the contents of another envelope.

"She's nearly seventy," Neddie said, following her own thoughts.

"She doesn't look it. But you don't look fifty. Maybe it runs in your family? Do I look my age?" Lindy turned her face to Neddie's scrutiny.

Neddie recovered the photos from their San Francisco trip. "See for yourself. You don't even look my age." She handed Lindy the picture of them both in the carved and glazed booth.

Smiling at the evidence, especially as she compared herself to Neddie's lined face and considerably grayer hair, Lindy said, "That's what comes of twenty years of drinking like you did."

"I like looking older than you," Neddie admitted.

"That's because you're hopelessly queer." Still looking at the picture, Lindy continued. "I wouldn't have believed that good looks would come to me with age."

"You didn't exactly start out with warts."

"I know. Maybe the warts were in my eyes."

Neddie held Lindy's face under the chin. "Your physical beauty is the least of it," she said seriously; then, changing her tone, she added, "you've aged like good cheese."

"Enough, you creep."

Neddie finished arranging a row of pictures chronologically. Her mother looked progressively heavier and older. The main symptom of age was an increasing dullness in Concetta's eyes; so marked was it that Neddie wondered if Concetta's sight were still adequate. "Do you think Concetta's afraid of getting old?"

Neddie's use of her mother's given name alerted Lindy. "She's in good health. She'll probably live forever just to spite her detractors."

"I don't mean 'Do you think she's afraid of death?' Do you think she feels less in command of things? Less able? Less important?"

"Well, she *is* less in command of things." Lindy did not add what a blessing that must be to those around her.

"I wonder just how self-sufficient she is. She was never very agreeable, so flattery is out. What must it be like for her now that Bobo and what's-his-name have all the aces, and she has to wait on their favor?"

Lindy smiled at Neddie's customary omission of her favored brother's name. "They always had all the aces, but frankly, I can't imagine your mother helpless."

"But don't you think Bobo especially sees through her manipulations?"

Lindy cleared her throat and organized the envelopes in the shoebox. "Want me to heat the rest of this coffee?"

"No. Put it in a jar. I'll have it cold. Should we go for a long walk or a short walk tonight?"

"Feel like going as far as the ocean?" Lindy carried their coffee supplies to the kitchen; Neddie went to the closet for her sweater.

"You didn't answer me about Bobo."

"I know. I was being evasive. Are *you* always able to see through a little social maneuvering?"

Neddie shrugged. "Bobo is a sap. He must think Momma has money and he'll inherit it if he acts the devoted son. You-know-who will get whatever pistachios she's got."

"Age doesn't necessarily mellow sibling rivalry," Lindy began tactfully. Thinking of herself, she added, "nor does it heal family wounds. Unless we make it our business to change, age only makes the original condition worse. If we had not changed our ideas of who we were and of what made us tick, we could never have stayed together. Of course the choices were so clear," she continued with the authority of a historian of emotional crises. "Change or rot. There's no holding the line. We *had* to change. But I don't suppose the choices are any less clear for those the world accommodates more graciously than it accommodates us. So many choose stagnation, thank you." Lindy shivered. "Is something bothering you about Bobo and your mother?"

"Nothing, I guess. I just suppose she'll be calling soon to convert me or criticize me." To Lindy's raised eyebrow, Neddie added the reminder, "She always calls a week or so after she sends mail." On their way out, Neddie made a show of fussing with the envelopes as she carried the shoebox to the spareroom closet. The studied nonchalance chilled Lindy. Foreknowledge of Concetta's pattern seemed to tap a reservoir of apprehension.

Mechanically, Lindy snapped on a welcoming light in the bedroom. She locked the door behind them, resigned to ending the conversation. Their walks before bedtime were ceremonial. Until the next after-dinner coffee ritual neither would speak of unsettling subjects.

four

Shaded by a trellis that supported the small vineyard her husband had tended when he was alive, Concetta sat erect. She was corseted and wrapped in a dark print housedress, the bodice of which she protected with a small square of white napkin. Methodically, she licked a mound of lemon ice. "If you don't come into the city once in a while," her son Bernardo was saying, "you'll forget what the real stuff tastes like." Concetta could think of nothing to draw her back to the city — leaving had been such a mark of prosperity. As it was, Jamaica was not far enough from the city.

Routinely, on the third Saturday of the month, Bernardo drove to the home from which he alone — unlike Carmello and Neddie — had gone to both junior and senior high school. Always Concetta led him through the dark, window-tight ground floor to the yard. There, if the weather permitted, they sat facing the overgrown vineyard; in winter they rocked together on the enclosed porch.

After an hour of visiting his mother, Bernardo invariably drove alone to a nearby shopping mall for lemon ice or Carvel or knishes. That trip would take as near an hour as he could in conscience pass and still satisfy his standards for the visit. Often he stopped for gas on the way. He reasoned that gas was much cheaper on Long Island, though it was no cheaper in the middle of his visit than in the early evening, when he was going home. Often he parked at the outreaches of the mall lot; on no other occasion did he prefer the exercise of walking. Listless about his purchases, he generally wandered at the mall, glazed by a window of stuffed animals, or a bubbling orange soda machine, or a display of shoes. Always he returned to Concetta with simple excuses for the delay. After their treats, Bernardo napped for an hour while his mother examined a recipe-diet-how-to magazine that he also bought for her each month. At the end of three hours, he took her to an early dinner, which he did not clock so long as food and drink distracted him.

Each third Saturday he told himself he would break the deadening pattern. Invariably, after Concetta led him through the dark house which always smelled of sautéed garlic and onions, he was hypnotized by memories. He was afraid to suggest any changes. Concetta was not glad to see him; his visits somehow lowered him in her eyes. Still, she would not tolerate neglect. He assumed his welcome was lukewarm because he was the second son, but it was never discussed. He did not want to risk hearing one of Concetta's tactless declarations of Carmello's superiority. She had made such statements before; she thought their truth was obvious to all and could hurt no one.

From the corner of her eye Concetta studied Bernardo's scarred and puffy face as he worked his tongue over the paper pleats of the lemon ice cup. He was broader in the chest and shoulders than his brother; he carried no extra weight, but he moved as though his body burdened him. He had been a boxer for more than fifteen years, winning no more than one or two fights a year, some years not even one. But he persevered in his career by changing his professional name regularly. What more Concetta knew of his life came through Justine, who had once repeated what Carmello had said of Bernardo. In fifteen years Bernardo had been beaten, fortunately, by only two or three fighters of rank. Not that he avoided punishment with his lesser opponents, but the shabby caliber of his defeats enabled him to endure so many of them.

Endurance finally won him the respect of his older brother, but that took years. During the most difficult, early times, Bernardo's win-loss record was a family secret. Not even Carmello—arguing, ridiculing, imploring, offering an opportunity in construction—had been able to talk him out of the ring. A heart murmur and a relatively late-in-life marriage had finally prompted him to provide more securely for his family and to end his career.

Concetta never understood why her son let so many strangers batter him. At first she dramatized her concern every time "her baby" fought. Those close to the family were surprised that Bernardo received special notice as the youngest of her children only in his manhood. The predictable outcome of his bouts taxed even Concetta's calling to maternal anguish. And Bernardo's losses did not provide the twisted dignity, however painful that might have been, which defeat in an actual affair of honor occasioned. Bobo, Concetta thought, turning the name over in her mind. Why would a grown man, my son, let people call him Bobo? *Patatuni!*

That was something Neddie understood! Concetta entertained a rare flash of approval for her daughter. Bernardo took money for fighting with people. *And* he did a bad job of it. It was a disgrace. That was one of the few agreements she and Neddie had ever reached by telephone. Concetta recalled the mixture of sadness and relief in hearing her daughter's comfort expressed in clumsy Sicilian. It was true that Bernardo did not understand the old ways. Neither did Carmello, for that matter. Both had effectively resisted learning any of the language. But hadn't she made every effort to raise them as Americans? After all, *she* was born here. With her sister gone, may she rest in peace, there was no one now who knew Concetta's mind as well as Concetta knew it. Still, it was a relief that someone understood, even if it was Neddie three thousand miles away.

"Oh *fa*," Concetta sighed.

"What is it?" Bernardo turned from the dregs of his soggy paper.

"Nothing. I was thinking of your sister." Seeking to avoid any further connection with Neddie than was implied by his relationship to her, Bernardo did not answer. He often felt unjustly classified with Neddie.

Disapproval of Bernardo's four-year-old marriage to a divorcee with children had been a convenience for Concetta, not a passion. She had resigned herself to less involvement with Carmello and Justine and their children as that family matured. She could not imagine having any importance in Bernardo's ready-made family. Maintaining the ordinary courtesies — when she considered herself beyond accountability — seemed to Concetta more trouble than it was worth. Had he married earlier, she might not have realized how unwilling to make the necessary social efforts she was.

She remembered clearly how Bernardo perspired and shook when he announced his marriage plans on one of their regular Saturdays. She had not expected or welcomed the news. Speaking of old world ways that she no longer observed, she said she could not, of course, go against God and openly sanction marriage to a divorcee. That must be Bernardo's private affair. She had supposed he would always be a bachelor. Concetta remembered how long she talked around the subject until her son's miserable shaking and sweating inclined her to admit that his happiness was important to her. She offered vague acceptance if he had to marry, but that could not alter her public behavior which, she claimed, was demanded by the Church. Bernardo's wife was, therefore, no more than a name: Lucille. But Concetta never spoke the name, nor was it formulated in her thoughts. "His wife," a pronoun, that *putana* — these were sufficient labels for the rare appearance of Lucille in Concetta's mental panorama.

Her longstanding discontent with Bernardo's monthly visits Concetta blamed on the marriage, which she assumed was unhappy, since it poisoned their Saturdays together. That conviction now controlled her thinking as mother and son drifted into silence. If that *baccula* had not been so thick, she would have come around after Bernardo's baby was born. But no, she had to have it her own way. Once, Concetta recalled, Bernardo did bring his youngest, his only natural child, but the baby was more than the hapless father and the unwilling grandmother could manage. Concetta could not imagine what kind of mother would permit an infant to travel bound and wedged in a canvas car seat. Concetta remembered her annoyance with Bernardo for surprising her with the baby. Even the usual dinner with its narcotic abundance was disrupted by the child's fussing. Purposefully, Concetta had acted as ignorant of pacifying techniques as her son was. Despite the vivid memory of that unpleasant afternoon — which Concetta had confessed to the priest; the child, after all, was innocent —

Concetta occasionally hinted that fate had deprived her of a grand-child. This fantasy disguised a longing for livelier company than her son provided.

At first Bernardo was grateful that religious propriety prevented the introduction between his wife and mother. In his pre-nuptial anxi-ety he would delay that meeting forever! So long as he was not ostra-cized. To his wife he repeated elaborate explanations for Concetta's limited recognition of their marriage. As each repetition put the taste of the lie in his own mouth, he soon realized that Concetta's unwilling-ness to meet Lucille or the children made no sense. But Bernardo could not tolerate his wife's clarity on this point. By slamming around the house and withdrawing into furious silence whenever the subject threatened, he avoided overt criticism of his mother.

He remembered feeling relief when Concetta assured him that his happiness was foremost in her mind. He would not consider whether or not he had been duped. If he had been, he did not understand how. If he accepted his wife's interpretation, he feared the shameful aware-ness of his own complicity. It was best, therefore, not to think of it.

Bernardo dozed in the afternoon sun while Concetta thumbed through an article on inexpensive ways to make room dividers. She snapped each page loudly, trying to wake her son. She wanted to ask what it was like living in the city these days. Did he think she would be happier there? Here, even to play bingo she had to be driven. Car-mello enjoyed driving her, but Justine often insisted on keeping the car for errands or to drop young Carmello somewhere. Justine made a big production of the distance from Jamaica to Rockville Centre; Con-cetta stopped asking. She listened to Bernardo snoring and turned the pages more noisily. Why does he bother? she thought. Isn't it just like sitting alone if he comes here to sleep in the yard? One of his snores woke him, and Concetta claimed his attention. "Bernardo," she improvised. "I've been thinking of selling the house."

"This house?"

"How many houses do I own?"

Bernardo rubbed his eyes. "Where will you go? How will you live?"

"Maybe I'll go back to the city like you said. So I can taste real lemon ice again before I die."

"How would you live in the city, Momma? Social security doesn't go far there. You don't even know people anymore. It's no place for an older woman alone."

"You'd be there."

Bernardo laughed. He was dimly conscious that Concetta was not serious, and he resented the tangle of emotions aroused in him by talk of an action she was unlikely to take. "Even the best old folks homes are out here."

"I'm not talking about going to a *home.*"

"Of course not," Bernardo corrected himself. "You have this home. You have tenants and responsibilities. In the city you'd be far from Carmello and Justine. You can take care of yourself here."

"I take care of myself because nobody wants me."

"Momma! What kind of talk is this?" Bernardo looked at his watch. It was forty-five minutes before he would suggest going to dinner; he had napped for only fifteen minutes. Irritated by being roused from sleep to argument, Bernardo lied. "I'm glad I woke up. I've got to go back early today." And once that was clear, the rest came effortlessly. "Lucille and I promised to take the whole gang to White Castle tonight for hamburgers and then to the drive-in. Some picture the kids want to see."

Concetta was silent while Bernardo re-laced his shoes. Go ahead, she thought. What do I care? Bernardo leaned over to kiss Concetta's powdery cheek. He was conscious of his mother's annoyance, but he was unwilling to coax her goodwill. She repeated his good-byes tonelessly, without seeing him to his car, but he gave no indication that this was unusual. When he was gone she carried both chairs into the porch and took her favorite seat in the cool, dark kitchen. She missed her magazine, but now that she was settled she did not want to return to the yard for it. Besides, she would not turn on the overhead light to read. From the fruit bowl in front of her she snapped a banana neatly and ate half of it. She would probably content herself with the other half for dinner. *"Your sister's* hamburgers!" she said aloud. "Always letting the children have their way."

•

The plumbing at Concetta's Jamaica, Long Island, home was more than forty years old when it required major repairs. A general contractor promised at least two weeks of upheaval and advised Concetta to stay with friends or relatives. This advice was more troubling than the bank loan Concetta negotiated to pay for the repairs and remodeling. Concetta consulted with Carmello about what needed to be done, and she followed his directions; but she resisted his invitation to stay in Rockville Centre. True, she would have the privacy of Angela's old room. Justine welcomed her, but Concetta did not want to leave her familiar surroundings even for a short time. She wanted to sleep in her own bed, eat in her own kitchen, use her own bathroom. She did not want workmen in the house without her.

One day, however, without running water, without the solitude and silence to which she was accustomed; the sight of exposed beams, rusted pipes, and broken plaster; the debris in piles everywhere — one hour of sitting in this ruin after the workmen left, frightened and convinced Concetta. She imagined rodents and vermin coming out of the holes in the walls, and she translated these imaginings into themes of personal and familial wreckage.

She did not phone ahead for fear that Carmello's offer of hospitality would be withdrawn. In tears, with a small overnight carpetbag, she arrived at her son's house. Carmello and Justine were shocked to discover that she had traveled unescorted by train and taxi. On arrival, moved by the condition of her home, she poured out assurances that she would be no trouble. Overwhelmed by the unfamiliar sight of her unchecked emotions and by their own good will, Justine and Carmello insisted on her unqualified welcome. The first night of Concetta's stay was governed by this mutual appreciation of need and generosity.

No one realized that success in the new circumstance was possible only if everyone was willing to change in unexplored ways. Those changes had been initiated the first night by uncensored immediacy; but by the end of the first week, everyone had returned to customary behaviors and attitudes. The tacit assumption that two women were now bound as one in the care of the home and its occupants stirred resentments and fear in Justine. She knew almost at once that it was unrealistic and unfair to expect Concetta to embrace domestic routines and methods not of her choosing. But what then was their appropriate relationship?

After a few days Justine decided to speak to Carmello about her anxieties. She had weighed his warning that Concetta could be with them for a while. Contractors were notoriously behind schedule; in old buildings unavoidable and time-consuming obstacles surfaced, and contingency repairs were necessary. That prospect inclined Justine to seek her husband's advice when they gained the privacy of their room. "I certainly don't mind telling her my plans when I go out,"

Justine whispered, when they were comfortably settled in bed. "But I hate feeling accountable when I'm away longer than I said I'd be. I don't remember till I'm across town that it makes sense to pick up the cleaning while I'm there. But I didn't think of it when I told her I'd be gone for fifteen minutes. Today I ran into Angela at the market, and we talked for an hour." Justine wound the hair on Carmello's chest into ringlets. "I'm used to more flexibility. I do what makes sense while I'm out. I feel uneasy about leaving her alone; yet, I balk at the idea of reorganizing my days to satisfy some social duty I don't even understand."

His arm around Justine, Carmello fingered the soft material of her nightdress. She usually slept without any gown during the summer months, but his mother's presence at their end of the house inhibited her. "Why don't you take her along when you go out?" It was with effort that he kept his voice low, unaccustomed as he was to whispering since Angela's room, which adjoined the master bedroom, had been empty.

"I did at first, but everything takes much longer to do if she's with me. To say nothing of the strain."

"What strain?" Carmello unwound his arm and adjusted the sheet covering him to the waist. "It's not as though she's a child that has to be watched."

"A child would be easier. I never consulted the children when I was dragging them around with me. We did what I needed to do. No diplomacy was involved." As Carmello made no reply, Justine added, "I don't want you to do anything about it. I just want your opinion."

"I think you may be exaggerating."

After a silence in which Justine weighed guilt against annoyance, she continued in a calm whisper. "How would you feel if you took her to work with you and propped her up on a shovel all afternoon?"

Carmello rolled away from Justine and snapped out the light. "That's ridiculous. There's no comparison."

"Of course it's ridiculous. What would you get done if you were checking every fifteen minutes to see if she was bored or tired or what her pleasure was?"

"Fortunately, there's no boss hanging over you, and there's nothing you have to do."

The long pause in which Justine swallowed the traditional insult to domestic duties passed, and Justine said, "It's not like you to be so dense, Carmello." And she turned away as her husband was turning toward her.

"Honey, I had a really difficult day today. It was roasting out there. And *I* have to stop at her house every night to see what those jokers are doing. Can we save this for tomorrow so I can get some sleep?"

"When tomorrow? Our only privacy is at this time. You'll be just as tired tomorrow night."

"Do you *want* to fight, Justine?"

"I want a hearing," Justine replied at the outer limit of her whisper. "You don't seem to understand. I'm not complaining about your mother. Confusing feelings are piling up in me simply because there is another person in the house with me all day. And I'm not used to it. It's not a reflection on your mother's *personality.*"

"Tomorrow is Friday. How about after dinner we drive to the beach and talk it over? I'll feel fresher without the threat of work the next day."

Carmello's warm hand on Justine's hip reassured her. Perhaps she had overreacted. Not since the children were small had she experienced so much tension in her work week. The possibility of being trapped again in those years frightened her. "I knew you'd think of something sensible," she said. "I'm sorry I was so testy."

The following day, however, Carmello did not arrive home at his usual hour. He phoned while Justine and Concetta were worriedly picking at the long-delayed supper. Just before quitting time, Carmello explained, the stonecrusher had fainted, apparently from the heat. In the fall he broke his wrist, and Carmello accompanied him to the hospital for treatment. They were still there. Carmello planned to drive him home as soon as he was released. There was no point in waiting supper; he would eat at the hospital.

Justine's morbid fantasies evaporated. So extraordinary was Carmello's delay that at first she completely accepted it. Only after she finished the dishes and heard Concetta turn on the livingroom television—effectively preventing her from listening to music, unless she wanted to use the radio in the kitchen—did Justine realize that her plans with her husband had to be postponed. All evening she rejected faint, but nagging, suspicions as unworthy of her. She went to bed early, exhausted by arguing and reasoning with herself.

By noon of Saturday Justine's anger was well advanced. Carmello had not yet awakened. Not only had he arrived home past the requirements of first aid, but Justine believed he was deliberately sleeping through the morning to minimize the time he would be obliged to spend with his mother. Carr was already gone for the day, and why shouldn't his Saturday be his own? Concetta, she knew, was at the television, though that house-dominating vigil had certainly been interrupted by a night of sleep. Tears of frustration threatened Justine when she heard Carmello pad from the bedroom to the bathroom overhead. Finally he entered the kitchen with a hospital-related explanation of the delay, and he went directly to the refrigerator. Justine watched him gulp from an already opened bottle of cola. Before she could stop herself, she said, "Use a glass."

"I'll finish it. I need something to settle my stomach." Carmello looked at the contents of the refrigerator while he listened to Justine move around the kitchen in abrupt, anger-collecting tasks. He knew she would regard their cancelled plans of the previous night as his fault. That certainty had inclined him to accept the dinner invitation of the stonecrusher and his wife and to enjoy their company and their liquor until after midnight. He had let the accident and its aftermath take up more of his time than was necessary because the conversation his wife had waiting for him was beyond his power. To him, his mother's presence was no more than an inconvenience. What did he know about the spite between two females under the same roof? Weren't Justine and Angela always at each other? Carmello ignored the fact that the memorable times Justine and Angela had argued were because Justine had interfered in *his* wrangling with Angela.

Concetta came into the kitchen to refill her coffee cup. "How can you drink that for breakfast?" she asked, as Carmello tipped the last inches of cola to his lips.

"He's hung over," Justine explained.

"I thought you were at the hospital with a friend."

"I was. We wound up having dinner and a few drinks at his house afterward." Carmello could not be sure his mother would take his part. He explained how he had been pressed into dinner. He could hardly refuse. He implied that the high opinion in which the other men on the job held him required his hospital attendance. He did not mention that the union representative had also driven to the hospital.

When Carmello tired of the equivocation, he said, "What say we all drive to the North Shore, and I take you both to lunch?" Carmello knew Justine would not show annoyance in front of his mother. She kept her back to him as she fussed with some unnecessary rearrangement in a cupboard.

"That sounds wonderful," Concetta answered spontaneously, and she left the kitchen to ready herself for the drive.

Justine turned to face her husband. "You worm," she said softly.

"We couldn't leave her here alone on such a beautiful afternoon," Carmello protested in a sheepish whisper. Justine shook her head in resigned disappointment. She realized it was *her* company that her husband was avoiding. She did not know how, or indeed why, to call this to his attention and thereby intensify her injury.

•

Concetta had had no adult experience as a member of a household she did not manage. Since she understood and could improvise behavior only according to rank, she misunderstood Justine's treatment of her. Concetta's view of family ethics persuaded her to see Justine's actions— courtesies Justine would show to any guest in her home—as deference due a mother-in-law. Nonetheless, throughout the first week of her stay, she avoided remarking on the hours her grandson kept or on the unhealthy food he ate. She resisted explaining her own household methods to Justine. She wanted to be agreeable. Now in Carmello's company for the weekend, rather than alone with Justine, Concetta was more relaxed than she had been all week. She waited in the kitchen for her daughter-in-law to finish her preparations for the drive.

Justine came out of the downstairs bathroom, which adjoined the kitchen, just as Carmello finished his second bottle of cola. "I'll drive," Justine said, taking keys from the kitchen peg. "Is everyone ready?" Justine's decision meant that Carmello sat in the gap between the front seats, but he made no objection. Concetta feared that the press in the front seat would trigger her motion sickness, but she said nothing. She could not very well ask Carmello to sit in the back, and it was out of the question for her. Without consulting Carmello, Justine followed a winding road to the North Shore.

Concetta listened attentively to her son's review of the work being done at her home. After returning once for clothes and other necessaries, she had been relieved to avoid the turmoil which, Carmello

43

said, grew every day. Still, she kept abreast of the progress and the delays. When that subject was exhausted, she responded enthusiastically to her son's comments on the roadside scenery. She had missed such conversation with Justine when they were out together. Justine was often silent and businesslike in the car, as though they were following a bus route and could not make unscheduled stops.

Finally bored by the sound of his own voice, Carmello acknowledged his mother's exclamations on the unremarkable with fewer and fewer words. He hoped Justine was noticing the landmarks of one of their early courtship drives. Hesitant to speak to his wife, lest she embarrass him with a sharp word or look, he tentatively rubbed the back of her neck. Justine did not encourage him by her posture, but she did not rebuff him either. He turned his body significantly to look at a roadside restaurant in which, years before, they had neglected shrimp dinners to gaze at each other. "I didn't have any breakfast," Carmello said. "We just passed a place — I'm surprised it's still operating — we can get delicious scampi there. Want to go back?"

Justine had no chance to acknowledge the conciliatory suggestion; Concetta said she wanted anything except seafood. Justine smiled at Carmello's discomfort. Concetta had no way of knowing that husband and wife were in silent communication. She had been the only participant in her son's conversation during the ride; naturally, she answered a question she thought was addressed to her. Justine continued to drive in silence. She was confident that the tax of making unnecessary conversation and the awkward interruption of their common memory would impress on Carmello the frustration she had sought to explain. She was also relieved that no question of fault or blame was involved.

After lunch they returned to the car through the parking lot of a steak house Carmello and Concetta had settled on. Concetta gushed thank-yous for Carmello's generosity. Justine was thoughtful. Preoccupation with the scampi she had not eaten depressed her. She told herself that concern over the expense of lunch, which she considered wasted on food she had no desire for, was small-minded. What difference did it make if she and Carmello seldom dined out? Wasn't it petty to imagine she had been deprived of some pleasure? Furthermore, she rarely ate shrimp these days. She considered taking the passenger seat, thereby forcing Concetta to ask for it, but once her motive was clear she could not act on it. She disliked bitchiness in herself.

44

She *was* tired of driving; she *was* willing to sit in the back. Why should she create an issue where there was none? From the back seat, excused from talking against the wind, she could dispel what gnawed at her.

Ignoring Concetta's approval of the seating arrangements as they climbed into the car, Justine was amused that Concetta went so far as to add that the arrangements were more sensible as well as more comfortable. Amusement, however, did not curb the hope that Carmello had noticed the tactlessness. Concetta wants her way just as I want my way, she told herself. Don't I often convince myself that my way is also in everyone's best interest? That's all Concetta is doing. Her hints are a way to encourage everyone to see as she sees. Certainly she's self-centered and inconsiderate. Aren't we all? Everyone — by which she meant herself — is not inconsiderate. Maybe Concetta is more selfish than most because she's more frightened than most? Recognizing her usual practice of explaining away whatever troubled her, Justine stopped making excuses for Concetta. She sighed and turned her attention to Carmello's question.

"I said," he repeated, "why don't we invite Angela and William for dinner tomorrow? Carr can spend a few hours at home for a change. We'll have a family dinner."

Thinking of the preparation and work, Justine said, "Who knows what William's schedule is like these days. Or whether they want the day for themselves."

"It's not every Sunday they have a chance to be with their grandmother."

"It's short notice, and we may not *see* Carr until tomorrow. Frankly," Justine surprised herself by calmly admitting, "I also don't want to spend the day cooking and washing dishes."

"I'll cook," Concetta volunteered. "It's been ages since I made a Sunday dinner."

The crankiness stirred in Justine again. Will you shop and clean up and make the arrangements with Angela? Will you use your charm to insist on Carr's unnecessary presence for his grandmother's sake? Justine listened to Carmello's enthusiasm for ethnic food she herself did not prepare. When she was directly questioned again, she said flatly, "I'm locking myself in my room with the papers tomorrow. Do as you please."

"Don't be a wet rag," Carmello coaxed. "It won't be any fun without you."

"No," she said. "Some other weekend maybe, but not tomorrow. I want the morning for myself." During the uncomfortable silence, Justine expected to hear the word *selfish* spoken aloud. She was by no means certain *she* could keep from saying it.

"Well, I appreciate the expense and trouble you went to today," Concetta said to her son. "It was very generous of you."

Is this really happening? Justine wondered, as jealousy pricked her. Alone in the back seat of the car, the afternoon breeze lifting her hair, she followed her thoughts. Concetta's flattery did not arouse a sibling jealousy. Rather she felt irritated by the challenge to her self-image as a gracious hostess and wife. She was surprised by the self-righteousness and insincerity she found underneath the self-image, and throughout the afternoon she brooded on it.

Justine's resistance to family dinner forced everyone's awareness that three adults, each with different, sometimes conflicting, needs and desires, now lived in the house. Justine knew Carmello and Concetta were suffering from that knowledge, but no more than she had already suffered. The following morning she argued with herself to stay in her room as planned. Still, her attention to the spread of newspapers on the bed and her pleasure in the strong, aromatic coffee was divided. While everyone slept, she had prepared for herself a tray that included a large peach and a wedge of coffee cake. Carmello's curt refusal to eat the food, which she had carried upstairs only as an excuse to use the tray, censored her. Nonetheless, she stayed in bed, though she felt imprisoned by her decision. After more arguing and worrying she kept faith with herself, refusing to bear responsibility for the household situation she merely identified. But the effort eroded her confidence.

She was showered and dressed when Carmello returned from his softball game. Downstairs, she greeted everyone cheerfully and gathered the food and supplies for their usual Sunday barbecue. She was pleased to see Carr loitering in the kitchen with Carmello, both waiting to be fed. It would be something of a family dinner after all.

"Entertain?" Carr echoed, astonished by his father's suggestion that he entertain his grandmother.

Carmello hushed him. "Lower your voice. She's been living here a week. Have you said more than hello or good-bye to her?"

"She's living here? How come?"

His son's oblivious freedom from household responsibilities annoyed Carmello. He explained the extent of the repairs to Concetta's house.

"What should I talk to her about?" the boy asked, slouching against the sink counter.

"You'll think of something."

Carr looked through the screen door to his grandmother, who was sitting in the same shaded chair where he had last been required to attend her. The ease with which he was able to pursue his own affairs, plus his natural good humor, made him willing to follow the infrequent directives of his parents. But he sank his hands into the front pockets of his dungarees as he looked skeptically into the yard. His grandmother's insistence on family hierarchy embarrassed him. He did not feel like the heir apparent, and he responded sullenly to her glorification of his position at the expense of his personality. "Was Granma always so . . . dull? I mean, her ideas seem so old world or something?"

Justine looked furtively at her son, whose skin condition, she was sure, would soon clear to reveal a scrubbed American face. He did not have his father's dark good looks — or her own for that matter. He was too earnest to be attractive in the same mold as his father. She had once described him to Carmello as hopelessly clean-cut. It had been a way to soften the fact that this son was not in his image or likeness, and there would be no other. Justine looked at Carmello, shoulders set to suppress annoyance, pouring his second glass of orange juice. "What are you talking about?"

"It's hard to talk to Granma. She can't talk about anything but family. And even that . . . she just gives pronouncements about how things should be. All I'm asking is: was she always like this?"

Justine remembered Concetta in the early years of her marriage. She had been full of pronouncements then too — a penny catechism on human relations, Carmello had warned. But as a young woman, Justine had attributed most of her resistance toward Concetta's ideas to racial and cultural differences. She had gradually become less frightened of those differences, but they had, nonetheless, permanently obscured whether or not Concetta had always been . . . difficult. She wanted to hear Carmello's opinion and was disappointed when he said to his son, "Naturally, you prefer your own pronouncements?"

Bony shoulders shrugged through Carr's white undershirt. "I doubt if I'll think of anything to say to her."

"In that case, just sit with her. She was with me all morning at the ball game. You can do your part."

"My part of what?" Justine handed her son a tray of relishes and paper products and asked him to take them into the yard. Carmello, she noticed, was huffing at his son's innocence and did not seem to be speaking to her.

During the pleasant lunch of grilled hamburgers and roasted corn on the cob, Carmello gossiped with his mother about his softball teammates, and Justine listened to Carr gossip about unidentified school friends. When Carr excused himself, Carmello pulled the chaise that matched his mother's chair into the sun, took off his softball shirt, and stretched. Justine disposed of the paper plates and returned the condiments and utensils to the kitchen; she then joined her mother-in-law and her husband at the shaded table. She felt drowsy after eating in the warm outdoors, but she sipped iced tea and responded to Concetta's remarks with the grace of long social habit. Carmello's rhythmic breathing dominated their silences. She wondered how many daughters slept through difficult or boring family situations. Aloud, she said, "Do you hear anything of Neddie these days?"

Concetta looked pointedly at Carmello. Neddie, like menopause or childbirth, was not a fit subject in his hearing. "She doesn't answer any letters," Concetta said conclusively.

"I had no idea you wrote to her. You don't know then if she's still with that same friend?"

"I don't ask about such things." Concetta folded her arms across her chest.

Nonetheless, Justine continued, "I've always wondered about her. Free to come and go as she pleases. She can live and travel wherever her whim takes her."

"It's a very selfish life."

"There must be some balance between doing for yourself only and cleaning up after everyone."

"What could be better than marriage and children? It's a sin."

Justine sighed, closed her eyes, and lifted her face to the sun. Have we ever talked of Neddie in so undisguised a way, she wondered. Since they had never met, Justine's sister-in-law was merely an occasional curiosity in her thoughts. She knew Concetta did not welcome mention of her daughter. Was she silencing Concetta by introducing the difficult issue? Justine listened to her thoughts as the sun warmed her, but she felt under no obligation to answer them.

Concetta's heart thumped while she excused herself for the half-truths she told about Neddie. She lied to close the subject quickly. She never knew what to say or to think about her daughter. After the first terrifying fracture to the values Concetta knew and understood, she had learned to avoid thinking about how Neddie lived. Concetta had lost the substance of her original feelings, and for that she was grateful. No matter how difficult separation was, Concetta never doubted that it was better than cutting herself open and looking for Neddie.

•

The third week of Concetta's stay found them all in the same chairs, after the same lunch, on an equally sunny Sunday afternoon. The only difference was that Carmello had been on the chaise for most of the weekend, sacrificing even the pleasures of softball to recover from a back ailment.

Sunday lunch was a peacefully reflective time for Justine. Sitting with her face turned to the sun, she listened to the spinning blades of a lawnmower and smelled the smoke from a neighboring barbecue. Free from the demands of the week, she enjoyed her idleness, the sunshine, and fresh air. This Sunday, however, she did not feel relaxed and serene; she felt vacant.

Sipping her drink, she contemplated the loss of physical and emotional contact with Carmello. Without his suppertime "What did you do today?" — and if she answered carelessly, his enthusiasm for a context in which he could visualize her — without his interest, confidence in her own views wavered. Not only were she and Carmello presently withdrawn from each other — even more in private than in public — but he was hardly the person with whom to discuss her current concerns. Reservoirs of anger she had never before felt magnified small incidents. She had not been sleeping well; as a result, everyone in the household irritated her. Without access to Carmello's judgment and opinions, Justine found herself questioning even her sanity.

Obsessive mental review of possible conspiracy whirled in her mind. In the past three weeks Carmello had taken his mother to dinner three times. Why did that entertainment, in which she was included, embitter her? Why did her husband's suggestions that their children participate in family activities with his mother curb her enthusiasm for any such entertainments? Was she unjustly judging Carmello's present illness? Or injury, was it? Relieving himself was the only movement he managed alone. He took all his weekend meals from the tray that she or Concetta carried to him; his appetite was intact. Was she imagining a connecting thread in merely circumstantial events?

Concetta watched her daughter-in-law sip from a collins glass. No wonder Carmello was cranky lately, with his wife drinking. Concetta had not noticed before how strained they were with each other. Living around a marriage day in day out, you see what you could not otherwise see. With relief Concetta remembered she would be in her own home in a day or two, among her own things, with no one to please but herself. Her daughter-in-law did not understand respect. But where was she to go if the bathroom stopped working and her house was in shambles? She had not asked to stay; Carmello had very nearly insisted. And they both — Justine even more than Carmello — made a show of welcoming her without conditions. Don't talk nonsense about staying in Angela's room all day. Enjoy the whole house, Momma. You're part of our life, Momma. Don't talk about being a nuisance to anyone. Hadn't she said all of that?

Who could guess that Justine would be jealous of the attention Carmello showed her. He, at least, made her visit pleasant. After work, naturally, he was tired and sat in front of the TV without talking to anyone. Even so, Justine said he seldom watched television, so Concetta appreciated his sociable effort to sit with her. On weekends he always suggested eating out or driving or making an occasion of his softball games. Justine, during the week, was full of shopping and errands and laundry and chores. When she cleaned the house, she rarely gave time even for coffee. And if she went out during the day, she sometimes ignored Concetta entirely. Being alone in someone else's house, Concetta reflected, is not like being alone in your own.

"I think I'm feverish," Carmello said, slowly standing and steadying himself. "I feel dizzy."

"You're probably logy from being on your back so long." As Justine spoke she kept her eyes on the hedges that bordered the yard. "Maybe you should move your chair into the shade."

"Do you want me to help you inside?" Concetta offered. "I can pull your chair over here under the umbrella?"

"I can manage, myself, thanks," Carmello sighed and hobbled into the house.

While he was gone Concetta positioned the lounge out of the sun. "I wonder if he'll get chill now."

"It's eighty-five degrees, Momma. He won't get a chill."

"But with a fever . . ."

"He doesn't have a fever. He's feeling terrible from sitting around for two days."

"Yes. What a pity to spend his weekend like this." Without turning her head, Justine shifted her eyes to see if Concetta were serious or required an answer. When Carmello returned to the yard, he stretched out with a groan. "Will you go to the doctor tomorrow?" his mother asked.

"I'll be all right tomorrow."

"But you're not going to work?"

"Of course, I'm going to work. I can't sit around all week."

Justine now turned completely away from the hedges to study her husband and his mother. "How lucky you went to see the contractor Friday," Concetta said. "Who knows when they would have called me?"

"He said they were taking the heavy debris out tomorrow morning," Carmello reminded her. "But that doesn't mean the place is livable. Or even that they'll take it out."

"The plumbing works, doesn't it?"

"Yes, I told you. The repairs are done, but there's a thick dust over everything. I mean everything. Even in the closets. You should hire a cleaning woman."

"I can do my own cleaning."

"You haven't seen it, Momma. These guys work like they were outside making a trash heap. You'd be sick if you saw the mess. Forget about cleaning it. Be grateful they finished on schedule, more or less. All it needs now is paint."

"They don't paint it? For all the money they charge, they don't paint it? How will I get it painted?"

"I'm going to refresh my drink. Either of you want anything?" Mother and son both declined. From the kitchen Justine heard Concetta ask, "What does it cost to get a bathroom painted?"

"Money. That's what it costs. I don't know exactly; estimates are free."

"If the walls are up, maybe I'll do without paint."

"The paint is not for decoration, Momma. It's protection. It seals the walls against water and dampness in the bathroom. You've got to get it painted. I wouldn't use the shower until you do, but you *can* use the tub."

They sat silently with the unpleasant fact between them. Carmello looked toward the screen door. He heard the refrigerator close, then a burst of water from the kitchen tap. "I can do the cleaning myself," his mother said. "But I don't see how I can do the painting."

"It's not ordinary cleaning, Momma. I'm telling you."

"But I can't hire both a cleaning lady and a painter. The cleaning lady will charge as much as the painter."

Feeling the contradiction of not wanting Justine to hear the conversation he was having with his mother, yet wanting her to return to the yard and save him from it, Carmello looked toward the screen door again. Concetta leaned forward in her chair. "Maybe Carr will do it for a few bucks," Carmello offered quietly.

"Oh, that's wonderful. Will you ask him for me?"

Carmello shifted his weight with a moan. "Justine is the one to get around him."

"Justine?"

"Were you gossiping about the absent?" Justine asked, as the screen door slammed behind her.

Speaking directly to his wife for the first time that day, Carmello said, "We were discussing the fact that until the bathroom is painted, it doesn't make sense for Momma to go home. There's no way to get a painter for Tuesday on such short notice. Momma thought Carr might be willing to do it for a few bucks."

"Carr?"

"If he could paint it on Tuesday or Wednesday," Carmello said quickly, "Momma could be home by the end of the week. If not, it depends on when we can get a painter. Of course that's if the workmen get out by tomorrow like they said, and the place is cleaned."

Justine tasted her drink. "Can Carr paint?"

"Anyone can paint. It's not even especially hard for a woman, what with poles and rollers and the new gadgets they have on the market." In the silence that followed, Carmello added, "Of course, there's no rush. Momma can stay here as long . . ."

"And you want me to ask Carr to do it? For a few *bucks* did you say?"

"You can get around him."

Perspiration accumulated under Justine's arms. The same beverage mixture she had been drinking all afternoon, tonic and lime juice, suddenly tasted bitter. She could hardly swallow it; her throat was closed. She inhaled several deep breaths before her voice was audible. "No," she said, prepared to explain herself. She did not at first realize that the justification was as naked as the decision. Her throat, however, was no longer gagged. Thinking she might not have been heard the first time, she repeated, "No."

The redwood chair creaked as Concetta sat abruptly back. When speech came to him, Carmello said, "I'm surprised at you!"

"Surprised?"

"No, no," Concetta interrupted, standing quickly to avoid hearing an argument. "Not on my account." She left the yard for the house while Justine returned her gaze to the hedges.

"I can't believe you're being so selfish," Carmello said, sitting up.

Astonished by the response of both her mother-in-law and her husband, with peripheral vision Justine followed Carmello's perfectly agile step from the chaise to the door of the house. She closed her eyes to the heat of the sun on her face, and she let the bang of the screen door seal her ostracism.

five

A bsorbed in the comforting familiarity, Lindy systematically washed, peeled, chopped, and tore greens and vegetables for supper. Her serenity was disturbed, however, when she nearly covered a piece of Concetta's stationery with food garbage. Without hesitation she returned the food scraps to the cutting board and recovered the envelope, but it was empty. Rather obvious placement, she thought, listening intently to hear if Neddie's breathing indicated sleep. Neddie did not always nap when she rested after work; and Lindy did not want to be discovered prying, but so far from the bedroom she could not hear any breathing at all.

She used the chopping knife to poke through the garbage; she looked in the livingroom on her way to check the wastepaper basket in the bathroom. She flushed the toilet without using it and ran water while she felt the pockets of the terry cloth robe still damp from Neddie's shower. Vaguely apprehensive because she had not been able to evaluate the letter privately, she resigned herself to an unrehearsed discussion of it at mealtime. Back in the kitchen, frowning at ingredients and utensils, she completed her preparations. When she was ready to toss the salad, she heard Neddie in the bathroom.

In cotton pants and a sleeveless cotton shell, Neddie came to the table; her eyelashes were wet from the water she had splashed on herself. She yawned and pulled out her chair. "I don't know how I did it when I was a carrier," she said, watching Lindy mound the salad in their bowls. "I prefer to think I'm tired from the heat rather than age."

They ate in comfortable silence until Lindy realized that though Neddie might *plant* the envelope, she might not volunteer anything further if it went undetected. Resorting to feigned surprise, Lindy said, "I noticed you deposited your mother's letter in the garbage. Was it that bad?"

"Ah, yes. My mother the letter-writer." Neddie chewed a piece of carrot as though it were the only obstacle to her having initiated conversation. "Can you think of any reason why neither of my brothers wants my mother to live with him?"

"Apart from their respective wives and children? Let me see . . ." Lindy did not like the question; nor did she have enthusiasm for ironical guesses, but she accepted her part until Neddie could warm to the subject. "The utter disruption of their lives? No? Surely there must be some good reason. How about the financial consideration of providing your mother with suitable accommodations? At least a wing, I should think. The emotional turmoil? Personal preference? Even those near and dear can be irritating occasionally. No? I haven't any sympathy with their hesitation. Has the subject come up? I can't believe she wants to give up the house."

"I don't know if she actually proposed it or if it's just an idea. I don't know what's going on. She said they don't want her even though she's not well."

"What's wrong with her?"

"She didn't say exactly. She spent nearly a month at Carmello's. Everything was not what it should be at home, she said, but she didn't specify. She's trying to worry me into a call."

"At least." Lindy felt capable of determining precisely what Neddie's mother intended if she could read the letter for herself. "Where is this love note?"

"I don't know. In one of my pockets."

Saturating a forkful of spinach with the dressing at the bottom of the serving bowl, Lindy thought in-one-of-Neddie's-pockets was not a promising sign of its availability. "She says maybe she should get a housekeeper or a live-in companion," Neddie went on. "The cleaning has been too much for her. But about my brothers she sounded resigned."

"Your mother resigned? I find it hard to believe. And a live-in stranger. That's a good one." Lindy enjoyed the occasional opportunities to say what Neddie would not or could not say about Concetta, but the verbal sport soured in her when Neddie, still mimicking and paraphrasing, continued, "What can you expect from sons? She says only women can understand women."

Lindy watched Neddie leave the table and take both of their bowls and utensils to the sink. She tidied the counter space and returned the unused salad ingredients to the refrigerator. With short wet hair, now mostly gray and silver, Neddie looked just as *obvious* as she had years before, when her hair was black, and she was heavier, and Lindy's parents had been horrified by her. Lindy recognized the acid in her thought. "Neddie, this is upsetting me. 'Only women can understand women!' What is she up to?"

"I thought you'd get a laugh out of it."

"It's very funny, if you appreciate gallows humor. But this letter that's too precious to show is starting to make alarming sense."

Nonchalantly, while she filled the sink with soapy water, Neddie said, "Why does it upset you?" The same sentence upset her as well, but she would not admit it.

Frustrated, especially by Neddie's apparent willingness to be obtuse, Lindy said, "Your mother is manipulating guilt in you. She doesn't care — and god knows, she doesn't have any idea — what a mockery this 'women understanding women' is." Lindy wanted to add: after all she's done to you, but she sensed Neddie's reluctance to hear any more. Such an emotional cliché — by which she really meant: after all she's done to me — would not have come to mind, except that the manipulation she suspected of Concetta was so naked it frightened her. She wondered if the old lady could successfully rely on this sop of 'women understanding women' to rectify her longstanding disdain, and then expect social forms to do the rest? "Does she think you're a moron?"

Neddie regretted inviting Lindy's comments. The idea that she had been *mocked* was disquieting. The suggestion that weakness toward her mother was the result of stupidity was unforgivable. She knew her susceptibility was suspect; probably any criticism of it would annoy her, but stupidity implied a lack more ridiculous than innocent vulnerability. "There you go again with that psychological bullshit," she said, hoping to distract Lindy from further probing. Her posture at the sink advertised that the emotions stirred by communication with her mother had taken hold; no further speaking on the topic was welcome.

Lindy recognized this rule of closure, but fear that Neddie was succumbing to maternal magnetism warped her good sense. In an instant that fear turned to indignation at the body language that demanded her silence and submission. She gave herself over — without realizing she had a choice — to Neddie's mood. Lindy's anger swelled as she re-experienced the suspicion that by not showing the letter, Neddie and her mother were acting in unison behind her back. Too many emotions converged in that instant, and Lindy was reduced to an expletive.

"Bullshit?" she snapped, focusing on the familiar complaint against her thinking in so unjust a context. How can the psychologically obvious be bullshit? Lindy's mind raced, but sentences did not come. She slammed a salad bowl into the sink, raising soap bubbles, some of which landed on Neddie. She looked for and found other unbreakable objects to fling into the water — a bulb of garlic, the pepper grinder, a wooden trivet. She wanted to split the work counter with her fist.

Silence exasperated her, but to deny the obvious when its stench is corrupting your very life, to pretend there has been no history — "Bullshit!" she repeated in stuttering frustration at her verbal amnesia. She waited for the relative speechlessness to pass, but it did not. Not only did she think an eloquent and devastating justification of her heat was moments from her tongue, but she also wanted to address what she thought was Neddie's condescending study of her inexperience with physical anger. Helplessly, she repeated, "Bullshit?" Neddie's head cocked to one side; the hint of a smile began in her eyes. The apparent composure taunted Lindy. "You fool," she hissed, forcing past the gagging limitation. "You stupid old fool."

She ran from the kitchen into the bedroom, no longer aware of Neddie's presence, but wanting, nonetheless, to get away from it. She bounced the bed with flutter kicks and punches. She feared she might hit Neddie or break something and was sorry she could do neither. Tears finally drained off the excess emotion. Presence returned. As she lay quiet, relieved of thought, she heard Neddie close the front door after herself.

It's your own damn fault, Lindy thought toward the door. She mumbled criticism and abuse, but was not sure if they were directed to Neddie or to herself. She knew that harshness and throwing things were unlike her, and she labored over the possible significance of such alien behavior. She wondered if Neddie felt so self-conscious after she punched walls and kicked things? She thought it curious that she was comparing her outburst with Neddie's more demonstrative ones, which began as pouting, but grew to full-blown tantrums when any effort was made to defuse them. Inevitably during these fits Lindy asked, "But why are you taking it out on me?" It was depressing to realize how often Concetta had been the real object of Neddie's emotion.

In the space that spent energy provided, Lindy now knew that Neddie's contempt for psychology had not caused the outburst. She had glimpsed, in the command of Neddie's posture, the bait she invariably took. She was as trapped as Neddie in the soap opera of mother, daughter, and unsanctified lover. Why had that awareness so tongue-tied her? Had anger, like Neddie's body language, been a defense against investigation? Had she stalled communication with Neddie rather than admit that she reacted to Neddie as mindlessly as Neddie reacted to Concetta? Couldn't she, who had words for everything, talk to Neddie about it when Neddie returned?

Panic paralleled resolve. She *was* sorry she had spoken to hurt Neddie; she intended to apologize. She planned and rehearsed an apology. She passed the evening discussing — with a fantasy Neddie — the part each acted in their repeated responses to Concetta. But no apology was made on the evening of the argument. Neddie did not return that night. Lindy tried to avoid concluding that a phase of disaffection such as dotted their relationship had begun, but what else could Neddie's leaving mean? Except for household details that indicated she had been home after work the next day but had slipped away before Lindy arrived, there was no sign of her.

Alone for the next three evenings, Lindy read and watched television to blunt her anxiety. Neddie's absence revived memories that pained her. Fear of infidelity and jealousy had been exorcised during their first ten years. She thought. Why then had she embarrassed herself that very afternoon calling around to see where Neddie was? Force of habit? In the early years when Neddie was a real trial, Lindy had kept a mental itinerary of her whereabouts; she felt thereby *in contact* with Neddie. Perhaps that's why she made the calls. Just to fix Neddie in mind.

Infidelity in the usual sense no longer troubled her. Lindy envied Neddie's ability to leave without guilt. The one time she had walked out on Neddie was unremarkable. She had been so filled with remorse for spitefully taking her stabilizing presence away from Neddie—in spirit, if not in miles—that she was gone only a matter of hours. Neddie was capable of more frightening distances. Leaving without explanation or warning, or some schedule of return, was at the extreme limit of historically acceptable behavior. Never had either dared beyond this expression of discontent. To press for separation, to dissolve the domestic arrangement—that was the only remaining step. And it was what Lindy feared.

Four days after the argument Lindy arrived home after school and knew Neddie was in the apartment. She went directly to the bedroom to compose herself, but she had no opportunity to speak according to any plan. Neddie entered the bedroom twice, knocking the first time and coldly excusing herself; she was in the process of carrying her belongings from the common bedroom into the spare room. On other occasions when one or the other had taken a solitary in the spare room, or eschewed their common bed for the couch during the years before they had a spare room, no such thoroughness had been necessary. All afternoon and evening Lindy was alert for ways to initiate a return to normality, but Neddie's manner did not simply make overtures difficult; it emphatically prevented them. Lindy, therefore, gave mental license to another troubling deviation from the pattern of former deadlocks. Boxes of her school supplies had been removed to the bedroom closet; and a wooden chest Neddie prized, which until then had been in the livingroom, was now in the spare room. Neddie had rearranged everything, making the room her own, as though she planned to be there for some time.

Three weeks of only necessary dialogue, of tacitly staggered meals, of separate sleeping quarters; three weeks without the companionship of their long after-dinner walks; three weekends without the restorative of listening to music together, or passing an afternoon at the park, or entertaining friends for cards or dinner — it all bode a more serious separation than either had dared before. What made it especially trying was Lindy's assumption, based on it not having happened for several years, that they had outgrown the need for such pointedly silent and individual re-evaluation. Faced with it again she was heartsick at the crevice opening before them.

•

On the last day of summer school Lindy came home unusually weighted down with books and papers. She tumbled the books onto the couch, stepped out of her shoes; and while the unimportance of the papers was fresh in mind, she crawled on the rug making piles of them to save, to discard, and to consider. Patting and squaring the stacks, she crawled toward the end table, and there she saw the letter from Neddie's mother. She sat on her heels and let the remaining papers slide off her lap. With both hands she re-twisted her hair. She looked mechanically at her wristwatch; she noticed a run in her stockings, which were exposed below the gather of her skirt. Sighing, she pushed herself up and walked through the apartment.

How gracious of her, Lindy thought, I can snoop without fear of discovery. Back in the livingroom, she took up the letter. Not only was mutual pretense of postal privacy jeopardized by the stupor in which she sat with the letter in hand, long after she had read it; the pose of self-possession which Lindy had been maintaining during the seige with Neddie was jeopardized as well. The letter included a decal of a religious figure. Surrounded by pets, she told herself, though she could have identified the saint by name. The letter was undated and without salutation or closing.

You get old you see mistakes. You push your only daughter out because how she lives you do not understand. You understand how your sons live but they do not want you. Everybody hurts you. You are afraid. Sons are for show. Your only daughter is for suffering.

Why don't you visit for so many years? The house is too big. There is room for you. And your friends. You must be tired of living in the country. So silent. Just like your brothers. Have you no love for your only mother?

"For godsake!" Lindy said, slapping the cushion with her free hand. "'Why don't you visit?'" The old lady's ability to make herself the victim of what she had done upset Lindy's sense of social fairness because it meant Concetta could play for what she wanted without the inhibitor of shame. Lindy's own shrewdness, she knew, was modified by a sense of dignity beyond which she would not trifle. She did not like feeling challenged. Helpless against her own thoughts and opinions, she replaced the letter.

I thought Concetta was fluent in English, she mused. Could she deliberately write as though to translate herself from touching immigrant emotions? I thought only Neddie's father was an immigrant. There was no way to ask about any of it, even if they were speaking. Neddie is always so touchy on the subject. Aren't there ways to help her keep that blood circulating without relying on family ties; Lindy felt the inadequacy that always discouraged her. Racial comfort was what Concetta could give that she could not. *Neddie will consider leaving me.*

Slumping on the couch, bitterness rose in her; still, she recognized the greater danger from her own swirling emotions than from the old lady's machinations. She could not afford the furious repartee she was conducting with every line of the letter. Nor did she intend to make the same mistake with this letter as she had with the last. She saw Neddie caught in the precious crisis with her mother. Certainly it was of her own making. She couldn't really be thinking of leaving me for Concetta! With momentary resentment Lindy considered letting Neddie flounder. Inarticulately. Alone. But Lindy's ironies kept inverting. Go ahead, she warned herself, be spiteful, and Neddie will surely leave. Without help, her mother will seem irresistable to her. And it will all look so noble. So righteous. Even strangers on the street might not make unpleasant comments if they appreciated her niche in family life. A dutiful daughter. How disgusting.

Lindy covered her eyes. She could not watch Neddie make that mistake. For herself she could not. Fear came with the realization that the silence in which they were living was already momentum toward Concetta. Lindy was disoriented. In *their* livingroom, surrounded by *their* common property, Neddie's presence was missing. Lindy looked at the sideboard, the dry sink, the desk — all furniture Neddie had refinished. Some of the pieces had been with them for twenty years. Impulsively, Lindy stepped over the stacks of papers and walked through the apartment again. Everywhere were the objects that marked states in their life together, accumulations that symbolized their harmonized tastes. She opened the small closet in the spare room and looked at the clothing Neddie had crowded into it. She touched a velvet jacket Neddie invariably chose for festive occasions; she noticed Neddie's shoes stepping on each other; the familiar uniform pants were on a hook behind the door.

In the common bedroom which had become hers alone, Lindy sank onto the bed. How would I live without her? With a roommate? And where do you find a roommate, a contemporary, to live with as effortlessly as we live together? Live alone. I suppose I could; others do. But I never have. What would anchor me? Teaching doesn't satisfy me as it once did. It's just a job. Important enough, I suppose, but living with Neddie is my life. The disorientation in Lindy's chest fluttered to her eyes, where apprehension swelled into tears. I can't let this happen, she thought.

•

Neddie, it was to be expected, did not appear that evening. Intuitively, however, Lindy saw her — either at the home of friends or alone at a bar they both patronized — safe from rash decisions. Lindy trusted her intuition, especially when it placed her under its automatic control. Influencing Neddie, even correcting their domestic variance, was not a power Lindy doubted in herself, if she chose to exercise it. And by suppertime she knew that she had indeed chosen.

Following that pensive meal, during which she had waited for direction to come with resolution, she washed and conditioned her hair. Shaking it dry with a soft towel, impulsively she turbaned it and retraced her steps to run water for a scented bath. There, absorbed in cosmetic ritual, she manicured her nails from a portable tray that spanned the tub. Now that school was out she treated herself to a colorful polish which, after application, she kept carefully above water. The residue of tension and anxiety floated from her. Feeling luxurious and purposeful when she stepped out of the tub, without toweling she slipped into the terry cloth robe that hung beside Neddie's; and after brushing her hair she went directly to bed. She read in bed only long enough to tire her eyes; then she slept in confident serenity, though she had no specific plan.

At three AM she was awakened by the sounds of locking up that attended Neddie's return. She regarded as a good omen the consideration Neddie showed by not turning on the hall light which flooded the bedroom as well as the hall. Sober thoughtfulness was also apparent in Neddie's effort to hush her exasperation when she bumped into the closet door Lindy had inadvertantly left ajar. Lindy heard Neddie's slacks, full of coins and keys, fall to the floor. The single bed creaked under her. In silence, Lindy imagined she could tell when Neddie's consciousness slipped into sleep.

After an hour of silent monologue, during which she convinced herself she knew what she was doing, Lindy entered the spare room and knelt on the floor next to the bed. As though solely for the comfort of the position, she rested her head on Neddie's chest and placed an arm across Neddie's thighs. Shortly, she felt Neddie's wakeful rigidity, but she sensed that Neddie would not jeopardize the comfortable body weight on her by any change in position. To Lindy it seemed many minutes before she felt Neddie's hand on her head, longer still before Neddie stroked and wove strands of hair through her fingers.

When it seemed they might begin the work of reconciliation, Lindy whispered distinctly, "Neddie? Your brothers aren't thinking of leaving their women for your mother's sake." There was no response. Lindy cleared her throat. "Remember a long time ago you told me how your brother, the one in construction, paid a lot of money just to buy his union book? Remember you said that, like us, it wasn't simply a question of 'paying dues' the way the young people say?" Lindy paused after each phrase to make her whisper intelligible. "Neddie? We have to buy a new book."

Darkness amplified the words. Despite the intensity of attention which Lindy felt, Neddie asked, "What are you talking about?"

"We have to pay the price of admission to life again because at our age there's a new set of problems. The old book no longer entitles us to anything."

"Did it ever?"

"Maybe just the security of knowing where we stood." Having chosen darkness as the setting for the conversation, Lindy was momentarily unsettled by it. She wanted to see Neddie's eyes, to gauge the effect of her words. Across the alley through the open windows, the soft speaking teased silent insomniacs. Maintaining the audible whisper, Lindy continued tentatively, "When we were celebrating my fiftieth birthday, do you remember telling me you couldn't believe they were going to let us grow old together in peace? We were drinking a toast . . ."

"I remember."

"They're not." Both concentrated on the nostalgic moment of privacy taken from their celebrating friends. Neddie had spoken from joyous incredulity. They had been together for more than twenty years at the time, victorious over the resistance and hostility that had threatened them.

"I'm so tired of this battle."

"Of course you are," Lindy agreed, assured by Neddie's tone that they had settled on the true nature of the conversation. "So am I, but I wouldn't straighten up now even if I could. And you! You think it's as simple as walking away from me? You think you could live in your mother's house, even without a woman, and be any less strange?" Lindy waited, hoping Neddie might protest against the thoughts attributed to her. "Your mother is taxing your heart for the oldest of reasons. You're a woman and you don't have a husband. That's *all* she understands. What other ties could you two possibly have?" Lindy shocked herself by adding, "Haven't you told me how upsetting it was as a child to watch her make up her face — like a mask, you said — and try to pass all of you off as something you're not?" Lindy's heart thumped wildly; she had not intended to say that.

"You read the letter?" Neddie asked, without in the least implying Lindy had spoken presumptuously.

"Nodding her head against Neddie's body, Lindy admitted that she had. She listened to Neddie's heart beating under her ear and calmed her own breath in its rhythm. "What do you lose if you stay in your own life?" she began again. "Nothing you ever had with your mother. She already thinks you're selfish and irresponsible. And you never grew up. And worse. Much worse. You know that."

"I believe she *is* afraid and that no one wants her. She doesn't get along with her *own* daughter; how could she cope with daughters-in-law?" Neddie's voice was pained. "She's an old woman."

"We're all old women," Lindy snapped, but she recovered herself quickly and added in the hypnotic whisper, "I'm an old woman too." She hoped that Neddie was not crying and that she would not. The confidence that had plunged her into speaking now seemed fragile; she did not want *to feel* the extent to which Neddie was evaluating her words. Such genuine deliberation confirmed that Neddie was indeed thinking of leaving.

"You and I hurt each other all the time," Neddie said, without quavering. "I know I love you, but love doesn't seem to make any difference."

Encouraged by Neddie's declaration, which had the sound of recent thought, Lindy lifted her head and spoke directly, "So we love no better than many others?" She placed her open hand over Neddie's heart. "When you were young everyone knew how you were. Things happened at the beginning, you know. I was still dating and being a proper young lady. You paid for both of us. I'm buying this book, Neddie. Stay with me."

"I don't understand."

"I know you don't. I didn't understand the crime against your early life. You understand *that.*"

"Yes, but . . ."

"Trust me."

With the proud bitterness that speaking of her youth always aroused, Neddie said, "You didn't trust me."

"I didn't make it easy for you." Lindy had completely relinquished the whisper. "But I lay down with you, and I'm still here." She relied on mood to dim Neddie's memory of how precarious lying down had been on some occasions. Also, by an effort of faith and will, she closed her mind to what, by analogy, she was taking on herself. The uncertainties she saw before her as a consequence of wanting Neddie recalled their turbulent early years, during which Lindy had frequently felt she had made a serious mistake. Could Neddie be expected to have fewer misgivings? Would she be any less of a trial on Lindy than Lindy had once been on her?

"I'm afraid," Neddie confessed. "The way it's been between us lately . . . I don't know what's happening. Everything is changing. I feel old and scared just like my mother."

"That's why I'm buying this book. I know it's hard for you, but you've got to trust me. Trust doesn't mean you're *sure.* It means you're not sure, but you go ahead anyway. To be ourselves we've got to change ourselves. I know it sounds crazy, but who are *we* going to tell about feeling old and scared, if not each other? And if we talk about that, we have to tell the truth or the whole can of worms will rot us. Neddie, let's be brave like we were when sexual desire made us brave." Lindy hesitated. If she repeated herself the argument would lose its strength. But if Neddie didn't understand or could not free herself from the mood, the outcome would be uncertain. Whispering again, but more rapidly now, Lindy added, "We have to be more queer every year just to keep up. Queer begins at sixty."

"You queer?"

"Just watch me." Lindy lifted the sheet and stretched alongside Neddie. She prayed silently that her conviction *would* bear watching. "How like us," she whispered against Neddie's neck. "Crowded on this uncomfortable bed when our perfectly conventional double is empty."

Physical loving was the obvious relief from the conversation. But they did not pursue their customary pleasures. Instead they pressed and kneaded and massaged each other slowly, thoroughly, relearning their individual and common properties — the knots in Neddie's upper back and shoulders, Lindy's angular throat and collar bone, the root-like singleness of their tangled legs. In the dark they gave presence to each other.

•

In the days that followed their reconciliation, Neddie and Lindy were reverently polite. They lingered together seeking a practical channel for their willingness to proceed. Their walks were often entirely silent. Sometimes when they returned home they held each other in bed until an earlier conversation could be agreeably resolved before sleep. One evening after supper they both followed the progress of a pocket of sunlight in the alley that bordered their flat. Shadows from the iron grille that covered their windows stretched across the table where they sat drinking iced coffee.

"These are the same shadows that chase me home after school," Lindy said. Her heartbeat was amplified as she waited for the courage to speak the truth that had been accumulating in her. "I must confess," she began, turning a coffee ice cube with her finger, "it frightens me and disheartens me that you're still talking about going to your mother's. I appreciate that we're evaluating it, as *our* decision, but I hope you realize my willingness to listen to your speculations is not encouragement. I do not endorse that decision. I don't know what to make of your assumption that I'll approve *any* decision you make. Unless you're really oblivious to the consequences some choices carry with them."

Neddie stuttered over an explanation, but Lindy spared her. "I know what's been true in the past. You decide and I make it work. But an emotional bond *and physical separation* . . .for some *men and women* maybe, but not for us." Neddie began again to defend herself, but again Lindy stopped her with raised hands. "I'm sure you'll come to this conclusion — at least I hope you will — but the route you're taking is tortuous. I thought your instinct would be surer and faster than your reason. I'm amazed at how much it hurts me just to hear you talk hypothetically about going."

"Will you come East with me if I make that decision?" Neddie asked quickly.

Lindy closed her eyes ceremonially. She knew the answer to that question, but she wanted to squelch the desire to call Neddie up short with it. Surprised silence followed her monosyllabic refusal.

Lindy knew the discomfort she felt was actually in Neddie. She saw Neddie's growing realization that the invitation merely scratched the surface of how little she had considered Lindy's well-being or the stability of their relationship. But Lindy was not eager to have exposed the extent to which she had been overlooked. She felt responsible both for the painful quiet and the single sufferer in it. The hesitancy of unfamiliar speech which had characterized her voice now changed. "Do you mean you want me to live with you at Concetta's?" she asked, unable to wait on the process of Neddie's thought. "Or do you want me to go East, find my own place, and live around the needs of you and your mother?"

Neddie wrinkled her face: how could Lindy suggest such things. But it was clear to both of them that Neddie had not considered any particulars. Neddie's wrinkled expression was not belligerent; the implications of Lindy's comments and questions simply stunned her. She was mentally running from her own judgment, but she already knew she could not out-distance it. The callousness of her mistake was apparent everywhere she turned. She wanted to apologize, but found no ready words to embrace her error.

Lindy could not let Neddie's realization grow along its own lines. Her fear of displeasing Neddie by calling attention to her shortcomings was more powerful than the success she was having in showing Neddie what those shortcomings were. She terminated another long pause with the suggestion that Neddie ask her mother to join *them*.

Startled out of the remedial awareness by the unexpected suggestion, Neddie left the dining area and waved Lindy to the livingroom couch. Carefully placing the tall glass of coffee on a wooden coaster, she settled in a corner of deep cushions with her knees pulled to her chest. "She'd never agree."

Equally startled by having offered a variation of the unacceptable situation she had summarily, but wisely, refused, Lindy said quickly, "I hope not." But as her confusion was intensifying, she added, "At least it's a more realistic proposal. We have our life here. We'd be together. You go back to your mother's and it's all over."

"What's all over?"

"Your freedom to be who you are *without constraint* on the only safe ground you have at the end of every work day."

"Oh. I thought you meant something else."

"I know you did," Lindy admitted. After a pause she continued through the fingers that covered her mouth. "*You* have been talking pointedly about making a complete and drastic change in our life together. For days you've been weighing this, wondering about that. Yet I merely observe that you are declaring the end of the line and you get an edge in your voice. Think about it, Neddie. Frankly, I was also speaking about my feelings for you. Perhaps I imagine you'll serve a missionary tour of duty and come back to me at its completion. Who knows? But I think you'd kill us by going to your mother's. I don't know if my feelings for you would survive the bitterness of your choosing voluntary servitude for yourself and do-as-you-like for me. *That's what's all over.* That certainty in me that I'll love you no matter what. Maybe you can blithely ignore me, but can you take an 'oh, that' attitude with your freedom and self-respect?"

Quickly, with the patient sigh of the wrongly accused, Neddie said, "You don't seem to understand what's at stake."

"*You* don't seem to understand what's at stake." There was passion, but no rancor in Lindy's voice. The formula of argument seemed to suit her better than uncharted self-examination. "With due respect for sacred maternity, you and I have been together for twenty-six years. That's longer than you lived under your parents' roof. Longer than either of your brothers has been married. That's what's at stake. Everyone goes through confusing emotions about the care of their aging parents. They don't leave their wives and husbands and families over it."

"You're on that business again." Neddie distracted herself with iced coffee.

"Yes I am. Will you tell me what makes your life with me so flimsy that you're willing to leave it for your mother, with whom you have never gotten along? Who is not ill, I remind you, just alone." Neddie did not answer. She replaced the glass and ran her hand through her hair in an effort to shake from her mind some essential of her problem that Lindy was failing to appreciate. "I know you'd never *say* your life with me is of less account than your brothers' marriages. But that's what the actions you are proposing come to. Your fantasy of belated respectability frightens me."

Neddie could communicate with as many varieties of silence as other people had tones of voice. But sometimes her silence was only the consequence of thought, the field of understanding. She was now wrapped in a silence which contained this effort. Far-reaching reappraisal was becoming an uncomfortable commonplace in her life. She was utterly dumb.

Lindy's assimilation of as much of the truth as she had been able to speak was unsettling her as well. Fear clouded her vision. She misconstrued Neddie's silence; and against anxiety she took the line of least resistance, which was the reassuring sound of her automatic speech. "If you feel a moral obligation to assume your mother's care," she said, staring at her feet, "I'll do my best to support you. If you wish, I'll help you write to your mother, or I'll plan with you what to say to her on the phone." She turned to look at Neddie. "But it has to be *here*. In our home. I will not trade off my life for her. And I'm shocked to see you, of all people, buckling under social pressure to be a conventional daughter."

six

Bernardo opened the gate to the backyard just as Justine was re-
moving fish from the outdoor grill. "Don't worry, I'm not staying
for dinner," he called.

"Bobo!" Justine received his kiss with her hands full. "You certainly are staying for dinner. There's plenty of salad. Let me put on a
hamburger for you. It'll only take a moment. I never buy extra anymore; Carr isn't often here for meals, and it just goes to waste."

"No, really," Bernardo answered. "I've just eaten. Momma and I
went for prime rib. If you don't mind I'll have a beer with you before
I start back to the city. Where's Mello?"

"In the kitchen. Come on. We haven't seen much of you this
summer. You look wonderful."

Bernardo followed Justine into the kitchen, where he hugged his brother, who immediately handed him a bottle of beer. "I saw you drive up," Carmello said, as he joined Justine at the table and motioned Bernardo to do likewise. "You were at Momma's?"

"Yes. We just had dinner. I won't take up your Saturday night. I wanted to stop in and see how everything was."

"Don't be silly. We don't have any plans. Angela is coming by later to drop off some crab one of William's buddies gave them. Can you imagine anyone not liking crab?" Bernardo could not. "Did Momma show you the new bathroom and moan about how much it cost her?"

"It was expensive," Bernardo said, stretching his chin.

"Did she tell you she was with us for nearly a month?"

"A month? No wonder she didn't want me to come out last month. I thought she had her horns turned. She said she passed a few days here."

"The time just flies when you're enjoying yourself," Justine spoke lightly, as she served from the large wooden salad bowl.

"She was a buster,eh?"

"She wasn't any trouble really," Carmello answered. Gesturing with his head toward Justine, he added, "They didn't get along."

"How is Lucille, Bobo? How are the children?"

"Everyone is okay and sends regards." Bernardo cleared his throat and returned to his brother. "I was wondering if Momma has been hinting to you about not living alone? Or about being sick?"

"Momma doesn't *hint*. She wants you to come around more often?"

"Not that so much. Well, yes in a way. Today she said I should call more often 'cause she could fall over dead and nobody would know it until her body stank.'"

"That's my mother," Carmello said, enjoying Concetta's crude picture.

"You don't check in on her every few days?"

Justine had been listening attentively to the two men and now discovered them both looking expectantly at her. She swallowed the last bite of bluefish, which suddenly seemed dry. "Are you sure you won't have some salad?" Bernardo declined. "Can I serve you?" Carmello also declined. Both brothers waited for the thread of conversation to resume.

"You don't think there's something we should be doing for Momma?" Bernardo asked hesitantly.

"If the time comes that she needs money, that's something we can work out. You, me, and Neddie." As always, Justine was surprised to hear her sister-in-law's name. She collected the dishes and worked quietly at the sink, as her husband continued, "But Momma doesn't need anything right now. She's managing, and she's healthy as a horse."

"I wasn't thinking of money," Bernardo said. "I don't know what to say. There's nothing wrong with her that she's not telling us?"

"Momma tells everything," Carmello answered, speaking louder than usual. "Over and above everything. You know that."

"I thought it was nothing," Bernardo said with relief, but with some annoyance he went on. "She holds on to the furniture when she moves around. Is that something new?" Carmello raised an eyebrow. "And today she says, 'I don't know how long I'll be able to manage here by myself.' I know she's getting old, but . . . what does she want from me?"

"She has nobody to talk to. She doesn't know what to do with herself. She likes to complain. Don't you think so, hon?" Justine offered a questioning exclamation that pretended she was completely absorbed in the dishes; Carmello, therefore, returned to Bernardo. "It's too bad Neddie ran off so young." Justine ran the hot water tap so long that the glass she was rinsing slipped from her fingers and cracked in the sink.

"She said you did everything for her while she was here. Treated her like a queen."

Carmello waved away his brother's words. "She exaggerates, you know. Did she really say she was here for a *few* days?"

"I'm positive. There was this other thing." Bernardo poured the last of his beer into one of the mugs Justine had slipped beside him. "Twice now, she talked about selling the house and moving into the city. Do you know anything about it?"

Carmello stood up and went to the refrigerator for two more beers. He motioned Bernardo to the screen door. "Come on, let's feed the mosquitoes. It's cooler outside." When they were settled at the redwood table, Carmello said, "What's this about selling the house and moving to the city? That doesn't make any sense."

"That's what I told her." Bernardo emphasized his words. "She said *I'd* be there. What kind of life would that be for her? She doesn't even know Lucille. Her sister is gone; she doesn't make friends."

"It's just talk. I'm telling you, Bobo." Carmello sipped beer directly from the bottle. "To me it wouldn't matter. She was no trouble while

73

she was here. A little boring maybe, but no trouble. Justine and Momma were another story. They were constantly scratching at each other. Justine's not over it yet."

From behind the screen door Justine's voice was muffled. "Do you want privacy or would I improve the scenery?"

"Are you finished what you wanted to say?"

Bernardo nodded his head to welcome Justine, but at the same time he gestured indecisively with his hand. "Come on," Carmello called. "I don't want to be stuck with this bum."

Carrying a glass of tonic and lime to the table, Justine arranged the chaise for herself. "Don't let me interrupt," she said. "I just wanted to enjoy the breeze and the company."

Carmello questioned his brother about mutual city friends; they commented on the standing and performance of their favorite baseball team; they expressed vague satisfactions and dissatisfactions about their respective jobs. Justine gazed at a swarm of gnats hovering over the grill. As the talk wound down, each followed individual thoughts, until Bernardo said he should be leaving. With a sigh, he pushed himself to stand. "Do you hear anything from Neddie?" he asked thoughtfully.

"Hear from her?" Justine replied. "I've never laid eyes on her."

"I forget," Bernardo admitted.

"Me too," Carmello agreed, standing and patting his brother's shoulder to ease their mutual loss.

Justine had never been able to loosen her husband's silence about his sister. In the early years of her marriage, she gathered every insight that might contribute to her complete picture of Carmello. Later, as the condemning fragments emerged, Justine was simply curious. But Carmello had been consistently unwilling to answer questions about his or his mother's relation to Neddie. He had, at times, been willing to receive Justine's comfort from discussing his disappointment over his brother. But Bobo after all loved and admired Carmello.

Now, witnessing both brothers' regretting the absence of their sister, Justine was actually pained; the sham accelerated new knowledge. Carmello's insistence on excluding his sister—even from childhood reminiscences—was *convenient* for him. Neddie could not be expected to increase his importance in any way. Relationship with her would have no rules or models; Carmello would have to *feel* his way through it. Neddie was not, as Bobo had been, worth the emotional wear and tear. Justine rubbed her temples as she sensed the favor Neddie had done for her family—Justine included herself—by moving her life three thousand miles away.

Carmello walked Bernardo to his car, and together they slouched against the front fender. As they talked they watched Angela park the station wagon and walk to the backyard. So intent was she in holding a basket of crabs at arms length away from her body, that she did not notice them, and they did not call to her. "You shouldn't let Momma know you take her seriously when she goes on like that," Carmello advised. "She'll just go on more. If you show you pay attention to her complaints, she'll have you coming around every week to take her temperature."

"That's really what I did," Bernardo said, taking his brother's tone. "I ignored her. But I didn't know if I was right. You always know how things should be. I feel creepy 'cause she's getting so old."

"And so cranky. Don't forget that. It'll work itself out. You'll see."

·

"Where's what's-his-name, my father?" Angela said, putting the basket of crabs down in the shade.

Justine smiled at the verbal tick Angela had inherited from Carmello. "He was visiting with his brother. He must be in the house."

"William says any moron can make *cioppino,*" Angela announced, sitting with fussy agitation. "I told him I was overqualified, but he should try. You'd think I refused to make his deathbed favorite. What is it with men?"

"Your father's aunt, rest her soul . . ."

"May she rest in peace."

"Always used to say that in this country you pray for your sons to marry Sicilian girls because they are the only ones trained to take care of the darlings. But she said you pray that your *daughters* marry anyone but a Sicilian—that being the life of a servant. William's mother had God's ear. It never occurred to me to pray over such a thing. William could be worse. He's very good with the baby. Your father wouldn't lift a finger to care for either of you."

"I don't like it when William gets into his Sicilian act. And *I'm* certainly not Sicilian."

Justine studied her own youthful characteristics reflected in her daughter. "Perhaps. Your father is. Make of that what you will."

"But it's only food," Angela said impatiently. "And it's too hot to make red sauce. And I didn't want to call Granma for directions. I think he insisted I bring the crabs over while they're fresh — 'fresh' he calls it when they're still alive — so Dad will see what a terrible wife I am. Then Dad will pull you aside: 'After all,'" Angela mimicked her father, "'what sort of daughter did you make?' Then you'll talk to me and presto: crabs for His Majesty. Sometimes I wonder what kind of a man I married."

"I often wonder the same thing," Justine admitted. It sounded casual and ordinary, not in fact the very subject she had been considering when her daughter arrived.

"Do you really?" Angela leaned toward her mother, as though mischievous gossip were coming.

"The only danger signals in marriage are your own," Justine confided. "Your husband's restlessness is nothing in comparison. I know how to make your father happy. At least I know how to give those comforts he *says* make him happy. But my own times of unhappiness? — that I'm powerless to alter."

"And Dad is no help?"

"Is William?"

Angela sat back and crossed her legs. Justine continued, though she noticed Angela's surprise. "Sometimes you know what's divided you." Concetta for instance, Justine thought, as she said, "Money worries, or another woman, or maybe alcohol. Something *outside* that starts a thin crack and widens as it goes deeper." Angela's eyes opened. "But even when you think it's outside," Justine gestured, "you suspect the narrow part of this . . . wedge . . . is coming from *within* you. And the damage is even more serious below the surface of what you can see. And you're the last to find out."

Justine was wounded when Angela — whether from fright or ignorance — shifted distractedly. Silence followed before Angela realized she should say something. "I've never heard you talk so . . . seriously," she said, her tone diluting the word *seriously*. "Luckily, you and Dad are not like other parents William and I see always complaining about each other."

Ashamed — first for having spoken, then for being ignored — Justine still would not compromise herself by assuming a happy face for Angela's peace of mind. She did wonder, however, if something was very wrong with her, because the complaints she had been gathering against her husband now included her daughter.

"William needs the car tonight," Angela said, standing. Her nervousness was more pronounced than usual in her effort to change the uncomfortable atmosphere. "I told him I'd only be a minute. He was so concerned that the precious crabs shouldn't go to waste." Angela took a step, felt the weight of false heartiness, and turned in sheepish confusion. "Mom, do you think . . . can we talk sometime? Just the two of us, like this?"

"Certainly," Justine agreed, but she knew Angela meant to hold them in their respective places. The conversation just passed would be erased from memory. Daughters made unsettling statements about marriage; mothers reassured. Angela kissed Justine, said good-bye, and was off in one energetic burst. Justine supposed it was a blessing that Angela had the attention span of a child. She did rather hope Angela would forget the conversation. With a sigh, Justine resolved to enjoy the balmy evening.

.

"Doesn't it seem that daylight will last forever?" Carmello said, straddling one of the short redwood benches and taking up the tepid beer he had left on the table.

"Tonight it does."

"Remember doing it out here after my party?"

"Yes?"

"Nothing."

"It's been a while."

"I've noticed. Something eating you?"

Justine sighed. "Something is, but I don't know what. Summer can be a sad time. Ripening is just a step away from rotting."

"A funny way to look at yourself, don't you think?"

Justine laughed. "I wasn't thinking of myself. Oh, I suppose I was thinking of myself some, but more about things in general coming to maturity. Our marriage. You." Quickly she added, "The children," though she had not been thinking of them. "Things like that. What our duties are to ourselves. To each other. To others." Justine realized she was speaking in the same manner that had just frightened off her daughter. "Did you see Angela?"

Carmello ignored the subject of Angela with a nod. "Looks like Bobo caught that duty bug too."

"Don't you ever wonder about those things?"

"No. Living comes naturally to me."

"The way you enjoy yourself always appealed to me," Justine admitted, drawing a smile from her husband. But the smile reminded Justine of what she had dreamed twice that week. In the dream Carmello was a smiling, handsome paper doll; large disembodied hands neatly scissored along the edges of his work clothes, hard hat, and lunch pail. His paper wardrobe included shiny black pajamas — such that Carmello did not own and would not wear. The accessory for his bedroom look was an erect penis which could be attached by two white tabs to the fly of the pajamas. Other cut-out props included a bulbous chef's hat, outdoor cooking utensils, a bat and ball, and a first son badge which, in the dream, hazily changed from a blue ribbon award into the flower prize that rings a race horse winner. No matter what cut-outs the sexless hands attached to the paper Carmello, he was smiling and handsome. The dream landscape was stark and disturbing; Justine had not mentioned it to her husband.

Now picking up the thread of conversation, she said, "Since your mother was here, I've been going over and over the question of duties."

"I'm going for a fresh beer. Want another drink?"

Justine shook her head. She accepted Carmello's unwillingness to discuss his mother with her. Systematically, she looked at the redwood furniture, the low fence that bordered the side of the yard, the full hedges that bordered the back, but she was unable to avoid the questions that bobbed in her mind. The echo of Carmello telling Bernardo that she and her mother-in-law were the cause of the trouble during Concetta's stay irritated her. He was certainly right about her definite refusal to undergo such a trial again! But Carmello was unaware that her insistence — which he never contested — released him from making any decision which might threaten his view of *himself* as a loving son and husband.

Briefly, Justine entertained a fantasy of Concetta as a permanent member of the household. In the fantasy Carmello came to understand his mother's flattery for what it was. Even so, Justine knew *she* would bear the daily misery of such a situation. She and Concetta. Carmello would meet what he thought of as his duties, but they were few and never conflicted with his personal comfort.

He's afraid, Justine thought. He's afraid of feeling wrong, or hurt, or confused, or guilty: ordinary emotions about his mother's stay. Who wouldn't be afraid of what looks like a choice between a mother and a wife? Why should he think he could avoid the problem? But he *did* think he should be immune from emotional stress.

Justine did not threaten herself with leaving Carmello if circumstances forced Concetta to live with them, but she knew intimacy with her husband would not survive that event. She wondered if intimacy — by which she meant not only physical closeness, but honesty — had survived the month past. Always before she had made allowances for Carmello's self-centeredness. So long as she lived for his welfare, they were in perfect harmony. But if the center of her attention wavered, their domestic life went out of focus.

When she tried to speak of these things she sounded vague, even to herself; to Carmello, she knew she sounded whiny. She could not accuse him of selfishness. What was the point? He was what he was. He had not changed very much since she married him. He still had the magnetism that made others, both men and women, turn to him. But he had grown to expect attention, and he was unhappy without large — Justine was beginning to think *excessive* — doses of it. She had been pampering a spoiled man. She closed her eyes on the subject which began to frighten her. She guessed Carmello was not coming outside again. Perhaps Bobo's sad reliance on his judgment made Carmello fear that *she* would initiate questions, the like of which recently had created some bitterness between them.

Some bitterness, she repeated, her thoughts not obeying censorship. As a result of Concetta's stay — that was it, wasn't it? — something hung between them. Justine did not want to say, nor did she quite think: my husband doesn't love me. But that was her suspicion. If *she* did not show love in familiar ways, he could not discuss any difficulties with her, much less show affection for her. Without the security of traditional service and respect, he could not show any weakness or entertain any possibility of change. But if the problem were artificial respect, where was she to begin explaining her discontent? "Saturday night in the prime of life," she said aloud, censoring her thoughts again.

"What?"

"Oh. I didn't think you were coming back." As Justine spoke, Carmello closed the umbrella that shaded the redwood table.

"You're sure you're not having a middle-age crisis sitting out here talking to yourself?" He went toward the garage to unwind the garden hose which was coiled on its green rack.

"Carmello? Sit with me a moment?" He returned and sat at the foot of the chaise. A pose of openminded innocence disguised his fear that Justine might be starting one of those conversations, frequent lately, that led nowhere and ruined her for sex. Justine felt his anxiety. "Never mind. You couldn't be comfortable sitting like that. I just wanted to be with you. Go ahead, water the lawn. I'll move the furniture and bring in the crabs."

"Okay," he said cheerfully, patting her outstretched leg. "Want to have *cioppino* tomorrow instead of barbecue?"

seven

N eddie tied the arms of a sweater over her sleeveless top and laced her walking shoes. Already prepared for walking, Lindy examined herself in the bathroom mirror. Their walks always began at the five-corner intersection of their neighborhood. Sometimes they walked the empty streets of the business and shopping district; sometimes they walked toward the cliffs that overlooked the Pacific Ocean; sometimes they walked from the five corners through tree-lined streets of detached houses. Their conversation could be animated, but often all necessary speech had occurred during the after-dinner coffee. In that case, they walked silently, looking at the exterior of others' lives. Only after dark was thoroughly upon them, along the cliffs or in the quiet residential areas, did they enjoy the exotic freedom of holding hands.

The route to the cliffs included an area of expensive homes. As they entered that neighborhood, the music and laughter of a Saturday night lawn party drifted toward them. "We could crash," Neddie suggested. As Lindy was silent, Neddie continued. "Remember how surprised I was when I discovered rich people had homes on public streets?" She waved a large circle with both arms. "All this is ours now."

Through the thick hedges and iron gates, Lindy regarded the homes Neddie's gesture included. "Your egalitarianism is endearing. Naive maybe, but sweet."

"We do have the run of the night."

"And the heavens," Lindy agreed, not wishing to dampen Neddie's mood. As an afterthought she added, "Sometimes you seem more at home in the world than anyone I know. But when I first knew you, you were like a displaced person."

"Should I do my urchin act?" Neddie asked, momentarily hunching her shoulders and lifting her chin. But sensing that Lindy did not want to play, Neddie changed her tone. "It's been no different for you. Sometimes you seem at home here; sometimes you don't."

"I suppose, but I've watched you more than I've watched myself."

"Everyone knows I've watched me more than I've watched anyone or anything else," Neddie admitted. They were far into the residential streets when Neddie squeezed Lindy's hand and slowed their pace. "Let's write a letter to my mother," she said, formalizing the direction their talks had taken. "We'll tell her how it is between us. We'll ask her if she wants to leave New York and make a new start with us. That's a lot to ask of her."

Lindy nodded, "It's also a lot to ask of us."

"What else can we do? It's the best *I* can do, and I want to be with you. With you I can stand anything."

"I know you mean that, but I wonder if you know what you're talking about? Do you realize it won't be easy? Every day with her?"

"In one sense it's like having a baby to keep a couple together. We have this duty, and we can test ourselves against how well we do what we're supposed to do. I don't think we're getting bored with each other or anything like that. But maybe we thought we were finished learning how to live. I don't think the duty is my mother exactly. I think it's *us*; we can't make the past last forever. There's more life in this direction."

"We don't get to rest, huh?"

"Not for long. Just long enough to get what we learn actually working in our lives, then we have to move on. Don't you think so?"

"I love you because you think like that," Lindy said, sobered by the magnitude of the decision they were making. "But frankly, it sounds exhausting."

"It is, in a way. You die when you use up your moving-on energy. But why would we save it? Look at all the people we know who stopped living in their thirties? Or forties? Or fifties? Just stopped keeping up with themselves. When my mother comes, *our* way will be stronger than hers. We will learn how to thrive. Maybe she will too."

The houses were behind them. A few isolated dots lighted the moonless horizon. Guided by the sound of the sea running against rock, they picked a familiar path through the low underbrush. "I also think it's the best we can do," Lindy agreed. Her heart's panic over the decision was eased. She realized she was not willing to issue the ultimatum: "It's Concetta or me." She could not live with that because she *could* envision other arrangements. Certainly they were idealistic, possibly foolish. But "it's me or Concetta" was the voice of fear. She accepted the realization ruefully at first, but as she and Neddie watched the ocean from the cliffs, she believed her inability to demand for herself alone was a gift. She squeezed Neddie's hand, grateful that so many years had passed in such good company. She knew that was no accident. She had chosen for herself a companion who expected her, encouraged her, inclined her to be the best of herself.

.

Later that week, while Neddie cleared the supper dishes, Lindy gathered papers and pens from the roll-top desk in the corner of the livingroom. Sorting the papers by handwriting, at Neddie's place Lindy arranged sheets of looseleaf on which were notes for the letter to Concetta. These notes had the useful simplicity of the temperamentally cryptic. Upside-down Lindy deciphered: *Don't be a coward.* Each of the sheets also contained two other ideas condensed from five or six lines: *Avoid guilt. Avoid feeling trapped.*

Lindy's papers were more numerous and denser with writing. Every sheet described a variety of fear. From where she sat she watched the back of Neddie's bare brown shoulders moving as she worked at the sink. Nowhere in Neddie's notes and never in speech had Neddie expressed fear of losing Lindy. She does not have that fear, Lindy reflected, because there is no basis for it. In my life, there is a basis for it. Neddie has shown herself ready to act first and face the consequences later.

Dressed in the cotton shell and linen pants that were her household uniform, Neddie came to the table and dripped a soap bubble on her notes. "Want to go for a walk first and do this later?"

"I'd rather go later," Lindy answered. "I like to hold hands when we walk; we should wait until dark."

"There's not much to see in the dark."

"Don't be silly," Lindy advised, pushing her reading glasses to the top of her nose. "We see lots every night. You're just trying to avoid doing this. Come on. It won't take long."

"Yes, teacher."

"It's true, isn't it?"

Neddie shrugged. "You first then."

Several methods of blunting the truth suggested themselves to Lindy, but finally she opened their second attempt to compose the letter. Writing it had proved so tedious that they had agreed to oil the process by describing their hesitations as they became aware of them. It was such a hesitation that Lindy now addressed. "When you don't agree with me, I feel afraid. If I can't make you see things my way, I get angry at you." Lindy noticed Neddie's nod. "You feel that way too?"

"I meant I know that happens to *you*," Neddie explained. "But I guess I do worry when we disagree. It's hard to think a thing all by yourself, but it would be worse if we always agreed. If you believed everything I believed, I wouldn't have any excuse for making mistakes." Lindy showed her disapproval. "I mean I wouldn't be able to tell myself I had to compromise to suit you."

"It doesn't seem like you compromise much."

"I don't. Look at all the mistakes I make. A little difference of opinion is okay with me. It helps me know what I think or how I feel."

"That's not in your notes from yesterday. When did you come up with that?"

"At work. My mind ticks 'round the clock."

"I made more notes this afternoon, too," Lindy said, pushing the papers a few inches across the table. She slipped into the casual authority that came to her with paper, pens and written assignments.

"You are working out something about your mother. Right? Well, I thought I was working out something about your mother, too. For you. But I'm really working out something about you."

"I'm working out just fine, thanks."

"About my relationship to you. About us." Lindy unfolded her hands to help Neddie understand.

"You mean about you?" Primly intertwining her fingers, Neddie mocked Lindy's borrowed hand language.

"No . . ."

"Yes."

Lindy was about to disagree again, but she smiled, and the misplaced patronization fell away from her. "Maybe I want a less naked way of saying it. All right. What else did you come up with at work?"

"Don't you think I did enough?" With fanfare Neddie took a small pad from her pants pocket and waved several written sheets in the air.

"I am impressed," Lindy said, pulling her chair closer to Neddie's.

"We're separate people who don't always want the same things," Neddie read from her notes. "Smart after so many years, don't you think?"

Lindy laughed. "What do all those other words say?"

"They say blah, blah, blah. The same thing. Except for right here." Neddie pointed to an illegible sentence on the note paper she held. "It says: *The one thing we both want is to feel right by our decisions.*"

Lindy had long ago learned not to discount Neddie's enthusiasm for the obvious. Whatever Neddie thought had consequences. Lindy's own thoughts and opinions were numerous and sophisticated, but often without practical application. As plainly as she had yet dared to renege, Lindy asked, "You don't think occasional bouts of remorse are preferable to the daily aggravation of having your mother here?"

"I can't live with that," Neddie sighed.

"If she comes here, I could lose you right from under my nose, as surely as if you went East. The oppressive subterfuge of every day resentments . . . I don't know, Neddie."

"You persuaded me — gently, but still you persuaded me — to forget New York. Me of all people shouldn't give in to social pressure. You used an opinion you knew I held of myself for your own purposes."

"Is that all on those little pages?"

"That's okay. Really. Because it reminded me that I *don't* ever want to give in to social pressure. I'm just returning the favor. Remember who you are. You have to decide for yourself what to do. Or maybe what not to do. It's simple, in a way."

"But how can you talk about acting according to a conscience that's governed by guilt? That's social pressure. If your conscience — or mine, for that matter — were governed by compassion, we wouldn't have this problem."

Neddie was thoughtful. Since her silent reflection could continue for some minutes, Lindy went into the kitchen to pour coffee from a large refrigerated jar. She popped two brown ice cubes into each glass and carried them to the table. Guilty conscience seemed to her the crux of the dilemma, and she knew she had explained it so that Neddie could not escape from it.

"Even if you're right," Neddie finally said, "and you may be, I'd still have to make that mistake for myself."

"But I'd bear the brunt of it too!" How *could* Neddie be so stubborn?

"You don't have to make the mistake with me. That's what I mean about not forgetting who you are."

"Maybe we should have gone for a walk first." Lindy held her head, but she could not concentrate. A moment of embarrassment, as though she had been bested in some maneuver, gave way to a sensation of bitterness. She covered her eyes and did not see that Neddie had moved to kneel next to her. When Lindy spoke, she was already wrapped in Neddie's arms. "Fear is the only thing that comes clear," she said. "I'm afraid of what's going to happen and how I'm going to feel."

"Actually, I've been thinking other things at work." Furniture blocked Neddie's effort to press Lindy to her as she spoke. "I know I take you for granted. I think you'll do whatever I want to do. Most of the time I don't know what *you* want. I assume you'll work everything out like I say. Maybe I confuse that with *knowing* you love me." Lindy turned herself more completely into Neddie's embrace without getting up and without disturbing the opening that Neddie's words created. "I don't know what changing *that* means," Neddie concluded. "It doesn't seem right, but I don't know what's right for us."

"I want to be with you," Lindy said. She accepted in herself, but did not say aloud, how dearly she was willing to pay for that company. That decision had been made days ago, possibly years ago. "Does this mean I have to give you up without a fight?"

"You're only giving me up to myself."

"It seems like I'm giving you up to your mother." Lindy took a paper napkin from the wooden holder on the table and sniffled into it. "Why can't you be having an affair like a normal person?"

Neddie pushed Lindy's note papers aside. With effort she stood up and pulled her empty chair knee to knee with Lindy. "We don't have the respect from others that comes with being married. Okay. But we've got an understanding. It lives and breathes and grows and changes because it's *ours*. We never know what to expect or how to act in any . . . official . . . family situation. True. But that's what makes us wonderful!" Neddie had been accentuating her words with movements; now she brought her open hands together in front of her lap and shook them. "We get to re-create ourselves every day."

"What you call re-create," Lindy said, squeezing her nose with the napkin, "I call having to fight for our lives."

"I can't talk for you, but I know I can't ignore my mother. Regardless of her tricks. Scheming is the only way for her to take care of herself."

"I know," Lindy agreed, restored to dignity. "Sometimes I think she's full of malice, but I know that couldn't be true. She's afraid. Just like me."

Neddie took both of Lindy's hands, closed her eyes for a moment, and said, "Today I came to another conclusion. Better late than never. My duty to myself includes a duty to us. It's suicide to think of giving up what we have for her sake — even if what we have is on the rocks. They're our rocks."

"You say the sweetest things." There was no triumph in finally hearing the reassurance she had sought. In fact, the ready irony with which she had answered was indeed bitter. "Why are we always *forced* to honesty? It's not as though we're virtuous. I'd lie to you if I hadn't made myself miserable lying to you at other times. I would lie to you if I could, you know?"

"I know you do your best," Neddie teased. "The fact that we're stuck with the truth is our magic formula. Now come on." By replacing her chair to its customary spot, she encouraged a change of mood. She pushed their previous notes into one pile and tore from a pad a clean sheet of paper for each of them. "Let's get this done." At the top of her page Neddie wrote: *Dear Mother*. She then stopped long enough to finish her coffee. Across the table she could see that Lindy had written: *Dear Concetta* above the words *Dear Mother*. Lindy's paper was half filled with writing, but from her vantage, Neddie could not see how much was lined out. "It's unnatural to write any letter explaining ourselves," she complained.

"It's that or be drowned in a sea of assumptions. We can't invite her without explaining the ground rules. It annoys me, too, that she doesn't have to write any letter to us as a show of good faith."

"I haven't been able to write a single thing."

"Everything I write sounds superficial and apologetic. I couldn't get anywhere writing as though I were you, so I tried to write as myself. That was worse. I wound up telling her how wonderful you are."

"She knows how wonderful I am."

"I don't think so, Neddie."

Neddie laughed. "I've forgotten what we're supposed to say."

"We're inviting Concetta to think about coming to live with us in the near or distant future — according to her needs. We suggest that she visit for a few months while her house is intact and see if she likes it here. That's the easy part. We also explain the way we live. That the essence of our life is not open to criticism or discussion . . ."

"We certainly do enough of that for ourselves."

"If she doesn't respect us as the main couple in the house, there's no point . . ."

"Wait a minute. We're not asking her to be a guest. We're asking her to live here. With us. Full grown."

"Then how do we explain what she's supposed to do? How she's supposed to act?" Lindy let the ballpoint slip out of her fingers. As she spoke she parodied her awareness that there was no way to command certain behavior or attitudes from Concetta or from anyone else. "This decision was easier to make than to execute."

Neddie sat gloomily tapping the blank looseleaf in front of her. "If we tell her how we live, that we play cards with our friends, that we go for walks, that the house is basically quiet, that we go to the movies or out to dinner, that we like to drive places . . ."

"Is she going to do all this with us?"

"She could. What do you think?"

"I think we have to make it clear that she's welcome to do any of it with us some of the time, but we need and want privacy — you and me —

to go off together or alone. Often. Regularly. *Before* the need to refresh ourselves makes us crazy. She won't know anyone when she comes, so it's common courtesy to help her feel welcome, but she has to make friends and live her own life."

"She used to like cards. I can see her actually enjoying an evening with our friends."

"If she can get over how some of them look, or talk or act. Or who they are."

"Don't you think she'd try if she realized it was the only way for her to be happy with us?"

"I don't know, Neddie. How willing has she been to make friends in New York? You're the one who says she believes anyone not related by blood or marriage is an acquaintance at best. I'm afraid she'll do a martyr trip, or worse, when our friends come. Sure, I can see her gossiping or complaining with some as the most natural thing in the world. She'd fit right in with the ones we've been avoiding, but let's be realistic, it would revolutionize her life. And do you think she's going to accept *me* as family? We're talking about her living her life among strangers. And these are strangers she has a prejudice against! She's going to expect a lot from you."

Neddie studied Lindy's eyes. She wanted to be sure that her dawning sense of what Concetta would naturally expect was free of Lindy's skill of emphasizing what suited her. "You're right," Neddie admitted. "But if she'd only let herself, she could actually be happy here."

"Sure. If the world were different." As the evidence of difficulty was accumulating, Lindy continued to hope that the idea of inviting Concetta would be defeated. Perhaps the effort to compose the letter would make obvious the inadvisibility of the proposal. If Neddie became convinced it could not work, she would let the idea go. Maybe not absolutely, but she might be willing to suffer occasional bouts of longing to have done more, rather than have them both suffer the daily predicaments of Concetta on hand for the rest of her life. See! Already, Lindy observed, you're being morbid. How she dreaded living together, and all the while hoping Concetta would disappear. Be precise, she told herself. You do not want to wish for the death of a member of your own household, but you're not sure you wouldn't. You don't know if you can maintain attitudes with which you can live in peace with *yourself.*

"What is the best we can imagine?" Neddie asked suddenly.

"I don't know. Along the lines we were saying. That she share our life, but she develops her own as well. And as a result of developing her own interests, we are free to continue our life together." Lindy laughed. "The best is that everyone lives happily ever after."

"Why don't we explain how we think it could be?"

"But it assumes we have mutual respect for each other. If that were the case, we wouldn't need to write the letter."

Neddie's enthusiasm wavered; she was silent again; finally, she said, "We'll write it that way anyhow. That's the only way that makes sense."

•

Woolen dresses, corduroy suits, and colorful blouses and sweaters covered the beds in both bedrooms. Every year as the fall term approached, Lindy emptied her closets and drawers and enjoyed a Saturday afternoon reorganizing her wardrobe. When she came upon the shoebox that contained Neddie's family photographs, she cleared a seat for herself among the blouses and sweaters that required the entire bed in the spare room. Sitting for a moment with the box on her lap, she watched speculations about her own family push their way to her notice. Ready to defend herself against any hint of guilt, she waited suspiciously for some emotion to possess her. None did.

The thought that one or both of her parents could be dead without her having learned of it was not a stranger. Every issue with Neddie's family stirred those and other considerations about her own parents which, otherwise, she kept in a corner of her mind. She knew, for example, that she wanted the vicarious satisfaction of Neddie's complete break with Concetta. But she had no intention of examining that sentiment. She had made herself inaccessible to her parents in circumstances that did not seem heartless, but the passage of time now accused her of what had been thrust upon her. Whenever she thought of tracing them to the home they owned, the home in which she had been raised, she censored any motive other than curiosity. And curiosity was not motive enough on which to act. Telephoning to see if they were both alive was obviously ridiculous. How could she begin such a conversation? How could she even identify herself? After so many years. Even if she wanted to renew contact with them. An admission of wrongdoing was inappropriate and inaccurate (though she *felt* she had done something wrong). She could not very well call to say she was willing to hear *their* apology. And if one or both were dead—it was not impossible—she intended to spare herself the emotional ambiguities. Whenever there was occasion, she systematically talked herself out of caring; she would not re-evaluate their estrangement.

Preserving the status quo enabled Lindy to harbor a comforting sense of superiority over Neddie, whose tangled family emotions she regarded as adolescent. *She* had no intention of embroiling herself in unresolved and ancient injuries. Having come this far without family, she would go the rest of the way alone as well. She disallowed further speculation, but was unsettled as usual by the memory.

A photo of Concetta and her sons was on top of the shoebox. Lindy stared at it. We should buy a dresser for the spare room, she thought. And if Neddie wants to refinish it we should start looking for something suitable immediately. There was no telling when Concetta would come, and Neddie could take months on a piece. As Lindy stared at the picture of the smiling, proud mother, she reasoned that Concetta would not come soon. Probably not even within the year. But she must be gravitating toward some decision. Could she be considering the trial period they recommended? That might mean this winter. She might like to escape the east-coast weather.

The three weeks of silence that followed the letter of invitation had concerned neither Neddie nor Lindy; they were not habituated to any regularity in Concetta's correspondence. Their letter had, in fact, encouraged Concetta to take time to consider the challenges of uprooting herself. This is no time for sit-down thinking, Lindy reminded herself. She closed the shoebox and placed it in the doorway away from her work. Returning to the closet, she organized items by color and occupied her mind with projected changes in her history syllabus.

Until Neddie spoke, Lindy was not aware that she was sitting on the floor in the hallway, looking through the shoebox. "Did you know that next week is my mother's birthday? Not the whole week, of course, though she would like that, I'm sure."

"You startled me. I thought you were watching the game."

"It's over. I was on my way out for wine to have with dinner. The pictures caught my eye. She'll be seventy this year. I'm thinking of calling her."

"I thought you might."

"I never wanted to make the first move with her. I figured if she had to tell me I was sinful, she could do it on her own dime. But her letters this summer don't even mention that. Maybe she's given up saving my soul? I thought it would be easy to call for her birthday and at the same time see what she's thinking about coming here. You don't think that's a mistake, do you?"

Lindy was not as tall as the dresses that hung next to her. She buttoned and arranged the collar of one as though someone were wearing it. The hesitation in Neddie's voice saddened her. "You afraid she's going to take advantage of you?"

"No . . . but will I be sorry I called if it doesn't work?"

"What sorry? I've been thinking along similar lines. Tell me more."

"I'm not sure. The outward sign of my not giving in. A perfect record of not taking the first step in case it turns out to be a mistake."

"I know *that* sorry. It's pride."

"Don't tell me that," Neddie laughed. "I'll never call her."

"And fear. Why do you want to do it? Her birthday is a convenience, isn't it?"

Neddie shrugged. "To put some personality behind the letter we sent, maybe? So it doesn't seem like a legal contract. When she comes we will have to talk to her. I have no idea what she's like on a day-to-day basis. Do you realize how many years it's been since I've seen her? I also want to know which way she's leaning. She may change her mind fifteen times; I know that, but I'm anxious to know what she thinks now. Today. It's a big change for us."

"You have a gift for understatement." Lindy left the closet, and with exaggerated moans, she sat next to Neddie on the floor. "Want to carpet the hall this winter? If we're going to socialize out here, we could make it comfortable."

Neddie took Lindy's hand. "We're good people."

"Speak for yourself. I for one am brazenly manipulative. Watch." She kissed Neddie with mock passion. "Darling, will you put the rest of the clothes away? I'm exhausted."

"Sure. What's the carrot?"

"I'll make a nice supper for us."

"You always make supper on Saturdays."

"Yes, but if I have to put the clothes away, I'll be too tired to make supper. You'll have to take me out to dinner."

"*I'll* have to take *you* out?"

"We'll go dutch, but that's my final offer."

Neddie leaned around the doorway on one arm. She looked at the clothes on the bed. "Okay. I can hang those. Color-coded, I suppose? Go rest."

"I'm too tired to rest. I'd better start dinner while I have the momentum."

"You call being crumpled in the hallway momentum?"

"You're so understanding. If I take a long rest, it will make going out to dinner so much nicer. I'd better lie down on the couch, there are a few more clothes on the other bed."

Neddie pushed herself up and offered both hands to Lindy, whom she pulled up and embraced. "Don't get too tired to carry your wallet."

"I suspect," Lindy said, heading for the livingroom, "that my fingers will be too stiff to carry anything."

"One weightless, large bill tucked between your arthritic breasts should do the trick. Beat it before I rebel."

•

Roused from sleep by the telephone early the next morning, Neddie sat up in bed and was unguarded in enthusiasm for the sound of her mother's voice. "No, we're not always in bed. You forget the time difference."

Turning in bed to watch, Lindy saw Neddie roll her eyes. She lipped: *my mother.* For privacy Neddie covered her face with her hand; she listened. Lindy poked her through the cotton quilt and whispered questions which Neddie ignored. She then tried to interpret the conversation from the fragments Neddie uttered. Was that *happy* . . . supposed to be "Happy Birthday"?

"I was going to . . ." Neddie began again, but her voice flattened. After another interval Neddie said, "Of course I don't think you're a charity case." Lindy stopped watching. She curled in bed and waited. Several minutes of listening passed during which Neddie interjected only monosyllables. Finally after two unsuccessful starts, Neddie said, "I don't want to hear any more of this. I'm going to hang up if you don't stop."

Lindy pulled the sheet over her head. She could not tell when

Neddie cradled the receiver; there was no audible good-bye. The silence grew between them. Lindy resisted impulsive comfort and questions. She did not want to irritate Neddie in any way. Finally Neddie slid down in bed, patted Lindy's hip, and opened an arm in which Lindy wound herself. "That takes care of that."

Despite the sensation of nausea, Lindy felt relief. "Come on," she prompted, encouraged by Neddie's initiative. "I want to hear the official word. Tell me what she said."

Neddie cleared her throat. "This Friday is my mother's birthday."

"We discussed that last night."

"Some people can think only of themselves," Neddie answered in weak parody of Concetta. "They need to be reminded. In honor of my mother's birthday, would you like to stop living in sin?"

"Are you proposing?"

Neddie continued in the same voice, "If I don't go to confession soon, not only will I die of cervical cancer . . ."

"That stinks."

"She didn't specify where God's punishment would strike. I'm doing some of her work for her. But she tells me — seriously, mind you — that your hand can wither from playing with yourself. Vision *is* impaired by self-abuse. She says I'm making myself sick. I couldn't get in edgewise that she was making me sick. Finally she says, 'Aren't you too old for your dirty practices?' "

"You maybe, not me. Does she have any idea what dirty practices she's talking about?"

"Who knows? I forgot the best part. If I don't stop this foolishness and pray for God's forgiveness, she will never again, by any means, contact me."

"You couldn't get that in writing, could you?"

"I think she's serious."

"I hope so, but I doubt it. Did she say anything about the letter?"

"Not a word. Like she never saw it."

"She saw it." Lindy's tongue and throat were dry. Her instinct to snap vied with her instinct to pacify. With less bitterness she added, "Maybe she really did think it over, and the ramifications scared her. You spoke in English."

"Strange, isn't it? She did too, mostly. Except to disown me."

"She's disowning you? Again?"

Neddie nodded her head rhythmically. "With curses that carry over to my children — poor babies. Thank god I listened to so many rehearsals over the years; she might have hurt my feelings." Neddie's voice wavered.

Criticism and commentary rushed to Lindy's lips, but she suppressed them. Efforts to be witty on Neddie's behalf might unnecessarily twist the hopes that now had to be re-buried. Against her better judgment, Lindy knew that she herself had imagined mutual respect with Concetta. In all likelihood, Neddie had dreamed an even sweeter reconciliation. "Are you okay?" Lindy asked, pushing strands of gray hair behind her ear.

"Even if she calls again, I'll be okay. Don't think I'm crying over her."

"I know. I know." Certainly she, Lindy, was not crying over Concetta.

After a few moments, Lindy controlled her tears. It disheartened her when she and Neddie were both crying at the same time. She tightened her arm around Neddie and prayed silently for the courage to face their own uncharted aging. She would guard herself and Neddie carefully for the next few weeks. With Neddie safe in her arms, she accepted matter-of-factly that they would walk over this moment. She fought with the desire to repeat a remark, more than five years old, which floated to consciousness. To open the tightness in her throat, inaudibly against Neddie's breasts she extrapolated the words of her fiftieth birthday toast: I can't believe they're going to let one of us bury the other in peace.

the end